# RAMBLIN' ON
## More Adventures in Paradise

by Joe Race

"This is work of fiction. Names, characters, places and incidents are either the product of the author's imagination or are used fictitiously. Any resemblance to events or persons living or dead, is entirely coincidental. To summarize, this novel is a work of fiction, except for the parts that aren't…"

Order this book online at www.trafford.com
or email orders@trafford.com

Most Trafford titles are also available at major online book retailers.

Cover photo of Uracus, aka Farallon de Pajaros--by Photographer Fran Castro
Author Photo by Paila Miradora

Note for Librarians: A cataloguing record for this book is available from Library and Archives Canada at www.collectionscanada.ca/amicus/index-e.html

Printed in Victoria, BC, Canada.

ISBN: 9781-4269-1109-5 (soft cover)
ISBN: 9781-4269-1111-8 (eBook)

*Our mission is to efficiently provide the world's finest, most comprehensive book publishing service, enabling every author to experience success. To find out how to publish your book, your way, and have it available worldwide, visit us online at www.trafford.com*

*Trafford rev. 8/3/2009*

 www.trafford.com

**North America & international**
toll-free: 1 888 232 4444 (USA & Canada)
phone: 250 383 6864 ♦ fax: 812 355 4082

# Other titles by the author:

Movin' On
Continuin' On
Ramblin' On
Moon Over Manila
Hawaiian Paniolo
Sitting on a Goldmine
Floater on the Reef
Christmas in the Tropics
The Korean Shadow (children)
Shrimp: The Way You Like It

# POTPOURRI & QUOTATIONS – ABOUT LOVE AND LIFE

**Aristotle** – "We are what we repeatedly do. Excellence, then, is not an act, but a habit."

**Alcohol warning sign in Palau bar** - "The consumption of alcohol may cause pregnancy…now you're wondering what the hell happened to your bra and panties."

**Anthony Pellegrino** (successful Saipan businessman) – "Change is the only reality we have. To live is to change, and to be perfect is to have changed often. Think about it!"

**Bar Advisement - Saipan**: "Never, I mean never…look into those big brown eyes…if you do, you will lose your soul!" (referring to Filipinas).

**Benjamin Franklin** – "You cannot pluck roses without fear of thorns, nor enjoy another's fair wife without danger of horns."

**Bette Davis** – "I'd marry again if I found a man who had fifteen million and would sign over half of it before the marriage and guarantee he'd be dead within a year." (same idea as the Filipina joke – "When you find a new husband, *Matandang, Mayaman, Madaling Mamatay*, i.e., marry a man who is old, rich and ready to die.")

**Calvin Coolidge** - "When he was President, Calvin Coolidge visited a farm in New England with his wife. On noticing a large number of chicks and thousands of eggs, Mrs. Coolidge asked how many roosters it took to do all the fertilizing. 'Not many,' said the proud farmer, 'Each rooster does his duty many times a day.' The first lady said, 'You might point that out to Mr. Coolidge.' The President countered by asking the farmer if the roosters had to limit themselves to only one hen. 'No,' replied the farmer, 'They have virtual harems.' Silent Cal asserted, 'You might point that out to Mrs. Coolidge.' Animal research tells us that a change of partner increases sexual interest and activity levels. A male animal can perform far longer and with greater stamina if his partners are rotated."

**Carl Sandburg** - "Time if the coin of your life. It is the only coin you have, and only you can determine how it will be spent. Be careful lest you let other people spend it for you..."

**Disraeli** – A member of the British Parliament said to Minister Disraeli: "Sir, you will either die on the gallows or of some unspeakable disease." Disraeli retorted, "That depends, Sir, whether I embrace your policies or your mistress!"

**Eleanor Roosevelt, 1945** – "The Marines I have seen around the world have the cleanest bodies, the filthiest minds, the highest morale and the lowest morals of any group of animals I have ever seen. Thank God for the USMC!"

**Falun Gong** – major Chinese meditation and peace group, teaching "Zhen, Shan, Ren," meaning Truth, Compassion, Forbearance (tolerance) in main book "Zhuan Falun."

**Gustave Flaubert** - "A joke is the most powerful thing there is (ask Cocina Parker), the most terrible: it is irresistible...Great pity for people who believe in the seriousness of life."

**Harry S. Truman (1884-1972)** – "It doesn't matter how big a ranch you own, or how many cows you brand, the size of your funeral is still gonna depend on the weather."

**James II of England (1633-1701)** – "Nothing has been more fatal to men, and to great men, than the letting themselves go to the forbidden love of women. Of all the vices it is the most bewitching and harder to be mastered if it not crushed in the very bud…"

**John Steinbeck (1902-1968)** – "An armed man will kill an unarmed man with monotonous regularity." (Second Amendment discussion)

**Lady Castlemaine** (mistress to King Charles – 1671) – She took on new, younger lovers and a witty verse went through the London marketplace – "Full forty men a day provided for this whore; Yet like a bitch, she wags her tail for more."

**Leo Tolstoy** – "Everyone thinks of changing the world, but no one thinks of changing himself."

**Lillie Langtry (1877)** – King Edward VII said to her, "I've spent enough on you to buy a battleship," to which she replied, "And you've spent enough in me to float one."

**Margaret Mead (1901-1978)** - "Every time we liberate a woman, we liberate a man…"

**Matthew 6:27** – "Who of you by worrying can add a single minute to his life." (Biblical front-runner of reggae - "Don't worry – be happy!")

**MLK Jr.** – "There are three words for love: *eros* is a sort of esthetic, romantic love; *philia* is a kind of intimate love between personal friends; *agape* is more than romantic love, it is more than friendship… it is understanding, creative, redemptive good will toward all men… it is overflowing love which seeks nothing in return. Peace, equality and justice depend on agape to define the ultimate morality of the universe…"

**Samuel Johnson,** lexicographer (1709-1784) – "Be not too hasty to trust or admire the teachers of morality, they discourse like angels but they live like men…"

**Sigmund Freud** (1856-1939) – "All love is transference, nothing more than two normal neurotics mingling their infantile libidos with one another."

**The Song of Solomon** – "I sat down in his shade with great delight and his fruit was sweet to my taste…his left hand is under my head, his right hand embraces me…"

**Thomas Jefferson** – "Do not bite at the bait of pleasure till you know there is no hook beneath it."

**Virginie di Castiglione** (1870) - *maitresse-en-titre* – Regarding Napoleon III, she said, "The more I see of men, the more I love dogs."

**Whoopi Goldberg** – "When you are kind to someone in trouble, you hope they'll remember and be kind to someone else…and it'll become like a wildfire."

**William Wordsworth** – "That best portion of a good man's life, His little, nameless, unremembered acts of kindness and of love…"

# DEDICATION

As always, to Miss Salve'
Who keeps the home fires burning

# ACKNOWLEDGEMENTS

My island novels would never come to print without the support of the usual gang of outlaws, fine people like Juanita Mendoza, Jeff Williams, Urbano Duenas, Bud and Donna White, Marie Miradora, Johnny Bowe, Cassandra Nelson, Donna Liwag, Daniel Hocking, Patricia Friedrich, Juan Del Nero, Nicky Nichols, Cassie Hamman, Alan Markoff, Nancy Nielsen, and my in-house cooks, Paila, Katrina and George. Ayee, carambra! I like those grilled cheese sandwiches on whole wheat toast with a side of boonie peppers (*capsicum pimiento*).

I'm often asked if some of the stories are true, especially the ones handled by Tom Parker and Carlos Montano at the Investigations Agency. Suffice to say, the reader must keep in mind that names, and some circumstances and places, have been fictionally adjusted "to protect the rights of the guilty," until their cases are adjudicated in court. There's plenty of corruption and incompetence in the islands. I believe some of the island's nefarious offenders watch our more scurrilous officials in Washington, D.C. on television, and learn from the most notorious in screwing with the taxpayers…and with their mistresses.

Mahalo also to my faithful readers. I appreciate your thoughts and insights, and please feel free to visit my website at any time with your ideas and suggestions <www.josephrace.com>. I suffer from *dromomania* (look it up), and know that Saipan is a great jump-off spot for traveling in Asia, the Pacific Region, and Australia. Meanwhile, slow down, beat the winter blahs, exit on the next off-ramp, find a canoe or plane, and come smell the plumerias and night-blooming jasmines, and breathe in some of that fresh ocean air. It's free for the taking.

P.S. - Zane Grey, Robert Louis Stevenson, Charles Darwin, Paul Gauguin, Jack London, Paul Theroux, et. al., knew of what they wrote.

# CONTENTS

# PROLOGUE

My name is Tom Parker, crime fighter and ace investigator, formally of the Los Angeles County Sheriff's Department. After winning a huge jackpot on the slots in Las Vegas, I decided to leave the "mean, violent streets of Los Angeles" where I barely survived as a patrol sergeant in South-Central. I found an old friend, Attorney Ernie Martines on Saipan, USA, and through his contacts, ended up buying a worn-down, beat-up, dilapidated 88-room hotel and subsequently starting a private investigations agency with my good friend and partner, Chamorro warrior Carlos Montano.

It's hot in the tropics and the touching of bare metal can singe one's skin. Blood runs hot and as a result, romance fortuitously came my way. I fell in love and married my hotel manager, Cocina, and adopted her three beautiful children, Annie, Donna and Anthony. Cocina hired a great crew you'll certainly recognize as the regular cast of characters at the hotel, such as Myla, Lola, Aubrey, Yoshi, Mario I, Mario II, Chef Guangman, matchmakers George and Jo, dressmaker Kaylene, Beachologist Fred Cannon, Tennis Pro Jonah, and Mama-san Chang and her girls. Brother Zeke and his new wife, Marcella, and business partner Arnie Arizapa, are still catching "the big ones" in the northern islands.

The eco-friendly hotel was running at near capacity and the private investigations work was building up. It looked like we might have to hire a coupla more hard-working detectives to handle the workload. We picked up several interesting new cases involving a corrupt governor, stolen dog meat, porno movies, ladies of the night on

Tinian and Saipan, recovered Japanese mortars; and spin-offs from our investigations involving masturbating nurses, potent sexy elders, noisy lovers, dangerous fishing habits, marijuana plantation suppression, love potions and "hot secretaries," a colorful boat captain, and felony cases that could take us as far away as the Caribbean and Samoa.

Saipan continues to be a special locale, but like anywhere you take yourself, I soon learned that home isn't just a place, or a dot on the globe. It's a feeling of belonging and having friends and family, and becoming part of the island community. It's being valued and free to be yourself, and to walk the beaches and soak up the sun. Perhaps it comes with maturity and a realization of what is really important to any human being. It all fell into pattern of completeness for me living on Saipan and marrying Cocina, and being an integral part of a blessed island community.

If you read the latest research about human longevity, it is becoming apparent that the sense of "community and family" is equally as important as genetics, good nutrition and exercise, in living a long, happy life, and disease-free in many cases. On the islands, the quality of life became more than a tourist slogan for me – it emerged as a definite reality. It happened for me, and it can for you. Book a flight!

And of course, some of the best days include the maximum satisfaction of still *hookin' and bookin'* the bad guys, feeling the adrenaline rush, and helping the victims find their way back to sanity.

# 1

## THE GAMES BEGIN

I was strolling along the beach, minding my own business and checking out the new seashells that the high tide had washed up on the shore. My reverie and meaningful work were interrupted by the "bugle charge" ring tone on my phone. It was my beautiful wife and manager of our Beach Hotel, letting me know that there was a worried local man in my P.I. Office.

Cocina said, "Oh hang on, Tommy, you don't have to hurry. Carlos just arrived and is talking to him. The man looks like he's ready to cry." With Carlos on the case, there was no cause for concern. He was competent and educated and able to handle whatever investigation came his way. When things start to turn to shit, I like him at my back.

"I'll be there in about fifteen minutes. I still have to check out the hidden cave a little bit south. With the tide receding, there will be a lot of shells washed up inside. One of my California buddies collects shells, and I told him I'd get him some unique ones from the Pacific."

"Good enough." She paused and said, "Guangman just showed up with a tray of fresh donuts and that Korean blend coffee. You better hustle if you want a warm one."

"You got that right. Carlos eats donuts about as fast as Guangman can make them. He's a human vacuum cleaner when he spots food."

Hmm…fresh donuts. I cut my arrival time in half, cutting through a copse of shiny bamboo trees on the side of a hill overlooking the sea..

I walked past our bougainvillea-covered fence into my office finding the Commonwealth of the Northern Marianas Islands auditor sitting hunched over and mumbling something about a missing 4.5 million dollars. First things first after the required handshake, I grabbed one of the last two donuts left on the plate and poured a hot, fresh cup of coffee. It was delicious treat after a morning beach walk, and of course, donuts have special nutritional and spiritual ingredients.

The auditor's name was Augusto Garcia, "Augie" for short. Carlos and I both knew him from several white collar cases that we handled while working temporarily at the Department of Pubic Safety for the then-commissioner Lois Harding. She had moved back to the mainland, and a new governor's crony had been appointed. The new boss, Joaquin Cruz, wasn't real bright or educated but he seemed to be trying hard to shape up the piss-poor DPS.

Carlos asked Augie to repeat his concerns. I knew Carlos was listening carefully to see if there were any changes in his story, and maybe looking for new information. Augie said, "The government owed a local businessman 4.5 million dollars from a business arrangement that went sour. The Superior Court ordered the Commonwealth of the Northern Mariana Islands to pay up within one year. As the terminal date got closer, the Governor, Ignacio Antolin, drew the money out by check, telling the director of a retirement fund that the money was urgently needed to keep the hospital running. The director believed the governor had the authority to reprogram money, and he knew the hospital was having difficulties trying to attract physicians and nurses, so he complied with the request."

I questioned, "No electronic transfer? That's very strange." Pausing, I asked, "Augie, how was the check made out? To whom?"

"The director had the check made out to the governor, who said he was taking it right to the bank for deposit. He did put it into the Oceanic Bank, and after it cleared, did a wire transfer of the money to an offshore bank near Greece. This is where it gets foggy. The Greek bank won't release any information about its depositors. The whole process took place over a period of about three weeks. No one brought it to my attention until I got an anonymous call over the weekend, telling me that I should check the disappearing money."

He continued, "I figured it was just a mix-up, so I went to the governor at his house yesterday to find out what happened. We've been working together for over twenty years. We're in the same political party. He had just left two days earlier, apparently on a business and conference trip to Hawaii. As you remember, his family moved to California about three months ago, supposedly for the daughter to go to college. I checked his travel documents, called the travel conference in Hawaii, and it appears that he never checked into the hotel or showed up for the conference. One of the DPS officers examined the flight records which showed that he flew on to Orlando in Florida."

Carlos smiled, "Over four million bucks will go a long way at Disney World."

Augie gruffly said, "This isn't funny. Saipan is about ready to declare bankruptcy and this stupid politician runs off with millions of dollars. A lot of heads will roll over this little fiasco."

Carlos countered, "It's not your fault. You found the discrepancy and are trying to do something about it."

"Somehow or another, I'll get blamed. The Legislature will want to know where were the accounting checks and balances for the release of that much money."

I said, "All that will work itself out later. Right now, we want to know why you're sitting in our office?"

"I've talked to the speakers of both houses of the Legislature and the Lieutenant Governor. They've agreed that we should hire you and get our money back. You can bring back the ex-governor if you want, but mainly we want the money returned."

Carlos said, "Look, I'm sure that you can't afford us. Use the Department of Public Safety boys. They can coordinate with other police units."

Augie answered, "Yeah, right! Most of those guys have trouble finding their own assholes with both hands. We need your help."

I said, "We love to joust with windmills and right the wrongs of the world, but we also need the bucks to pay our bills and have a little spending money for hand-rolled Filipino cigars and Mexico tequila, you know the finer things in life."

Augie finally managed to smile and jokingly asked, "How about gorgeous, statuesque females?"

Carlos said, "Yeah, we'd like that too, but our wives are adamant about our monogamy."

"Okay, what's your fee?"

I said, "Per diem money, and twenty percent of the recovery."

"I can't authorize that much...way too high." He looked away, a sure sign that he was bluffing.

Carlos said, "No problem. Go back and talk to the big boys, and let us know. If it happens, we want a contract which we'll run past our loophole specialist, Attorney Ernie Martines."

Augie squirmed in his chair and said, "Okay then, I'm authorized to go ten per cent and per diem, but no more."

I said, "Nope, not enough. If you did your research before you got here, you know that the twenty percent is our standard fee, and that applies only to what is confiscated and returned, not the whole missing amount. With previous small recoveries, we nearly went belly-up on a coupla of our jobs."

Carlos asserted, "Take it or leave it. If you want, you can go to the private investigations agencies on Guam or even Hawaii."

"You know we don't want the loss made public or people from other islands covering up our mess. You got me, so twenty percent it is. I'll draw up the papers through one of our government lawyers."

I said, "Haggling is one of the things we do best. Let us know when you're ready. Have another donut?"

Augie answered, "Can't eat another one. They're delicious but I've already got heartburn."

Carlos said, "Tom, losing millions will do that." Augie ambled out, shoulders slumped.

"I just can't imagine the retirement guy cutting a government check directly to the governor. *Credo quia absurdum!*"

"Yeah, that too."

# 2

## INITIAL FINDINGS

Anyone who watched television or read the newspapers knew that Governor Ignacio Antolin was way over his head in trying to manage the Commonwealth. He had been a go-between for the foreign investors with the local people and had won over sizable long-term leases on property and jobs for his friends and relatives. He was a hand-shaker, a story teller, a bullshit artist, and a barfly, and was always able to fix up the investors with a golf game or a woman for the night, or both. He found his own wife in one of the bars that he sponsored.

Ignacio curried favors on both sides of the equation and when it was election time, the investors made sizable donations to the campaign, and the locals gave him their votes. Status quo was acceptable when the tourist industry was at the apex, but when everything started to plummet during bad economic times, there was less money to run the labor-bloated government, and he was overwhelmed. He was not educated or sophisticated, and he was basically running the government into bankruptcy. He was afraid to lay anybody off – any good manager would have realized the necessity of being smart for the long run. He didn't know the acronym RIF. The commonwealth was headed for a payless payday. The money was running out. The common joke was he didn't have a violin but could probably stroke out a tune on the ukulele while Saipan was sliding into Davy's Locker.

Carlos said, "The Commonwealth is probably better off with him gone. He didn't know what the fuck he was doing."

I commented, "The Lieutenant Governor is even worse. He's under federal indictment most of the time for a variety of crimes. Be nice if we could get some of that missing money back for the people. It's not much but would help with the old people and the hospital, maybe the schools."

"I put my feelers out, and found out that he has relatives in California besides his wife and daughter, a first cousin in Atlanta, Georgia, and also a brother in Fiji. He is part-Carolinian which means he has relatives in the Caroline Islands, like maybe on Pohnpei or Chuuk. In the island cultures, it doesn't matter how distant your relationship is, you're still part of the family, and the family will cover for you, particularly if you buy some rice and chicken for the table."

"Carlos, the mainland investigations won't be a problem. I've got police friends in all the states and they'll be glad to check out the houses to see if he's there." I continued, "We know the island records systems are not hooked up to the mainland, so I did a quick check with my LA buddies, and found that our illustrious governor was busted for drunk driving and also for theft in a department store. Of course, none of this is on his record in Saipan." I kept flipping through my notes for more information.

"Hell, he used to travel to the Philippines all the time and to Japan. Wonder if he has criminal records there also?"

"Probably. The fool drinks a lot and he's made loads of 'official' trips to foreign countries. Let me have the mainland addresses, and I'll ask my buddies to do some checks." I thought maybe through my international contacts that I could probably check out Ignacio's activities in other countries.

I emailed my police amigos in Los Angeles and Atlanta. They found the relatives okay, but not Ignacio, nor did they ascertain his whereabouts. The wife and daughter had moved to Santa Barbara, and seemed sincerely distressed that he had disappeared. The wife said he had been depressed about the job, and had left him because of his heavy drinking and his abusive behavior. He got so blasted one night that he forgot that his wife was home, and actually walked a whore upstairs to their bedroom.

The wife had a far-out theory that someone had blackmailed him and forced him to take the missing millions, and then murdered him. She said that he was lot of things in life but not a thief. She said that he often talked about returning to a simple life as a fisherman or a farmer, like his father, that he had learned as a teenager working along the hardy, sea-going men.

The wife gave the California officers several names of relatives on the outer islands in Micronesia. Besides Pohnpei and Chuuk, she thought he might have gone and lived in a shack on an island north of Saipan, a volcanic island called Pagan. But a quick check with immigration showed that he had not re-entered the commonwealth, and the Coast Guard hadn't seen any unidentified vessels cruising or landing in the northern islands. A radio check with the Pagan residents revealed negative results about his presence.

Auditor Augie Garcia gave us the first draft of the proposed contract. Ernie took a quick look at the small print and red-lined several questionable requirements, and we sent it back. It was a cut-and-dry situation requiring only simple language and not a bunch of "where as' and wherefores." We explained to Augie that time was of the essence, and we needed to get moving or the money would be buried so deep in international off-shore banking that it would be gone forever. He promised to get back to us in a several days. We had already lost important time in debating over the contract, not counting the days that Ignacio was already on the run.

Meanwhile, Saipan fell back into its hypnotic routine, and the contract for services moved from desk-to-desk at a typical snail's pace, like on a very cold winter's day and the snail was locked in ice. Time was slipping away.

# 3

---

# THE KIDDIES AND THEIR PETS

All children love pets. They don't necessarily want to feed them regularly or pick up after them, but they love the cuddling and companionship. Our brood of three, Annie, Donna and Anthony were just like every kid in the world; but there was major problem in that we lived on the top floor of our hotel in the penthouse. There was a standard hotel rule of "No Pets" and if some of the guests showed up with their cats or dogs, we had an adequate boarding kennel for their pets nearby. There was also a running area for the animals for their daily runabout.

A few obstacles to not having a pet were just exercises in ingenuity for our children. On one of her hikes, Annie found an old boonie dog that lived in the jungle near the hotel. She eponymously named him Bruno after one of our favorite piano players on the island. Bruno, the dog, had his own built-in alarm clock. Every morning when Annie came down to go to school with his breakfast, he was right on time at the jungle's edge, wagging his tail and playing the clown. He did the same routine eight hours later when Annie came back from school and gave him a plate of leftover lunches from the cafeteria. I saw him a dozen times and I would wager that that dog could actually smile. He was a lovable mutt and got a bad case of the mange, but Annie nursed him well with some powders and internal medicine.

Donna made friends with a feral cat that liked to whine outside the hotel windows. She called him "Fur Ball" and that feline learned real fast where her next meal was coming from. If you looked her directly in the eye, she had you hooked for life, especially when she gave her best sad, hungry look. She was a noisy, romantic little critter and kept propagating. On her second litter of kittens and seeing the little ones run over by cars or dying of disease, we took her down to PAWS and had her neutered.

Anthony's little friends were the closest thing to self-contained pets that you can find on a remote island. The neighbor's young rooster liked to come over to the edge of the hotel and dig in the dirt, trying to find whatever he could like natural seeds or some trash that someone might have dropped. He would absolutely go wacko, squawking and kicking up dirt, if he found a McDonald's bag, sensing there might be leftover fries inside. Anthony called him "Scratchy," and for good reason. Our gardener, Yoshi, would see him scratching in the dirt, and say that he had to devise a way to get that chicken digging up the weeds in the orchids.

Another one of Anthony's little friend was a seven-inch lizard that he called "Georgie Gecko." Georgie was the champion mosquito catcher of all time. His tongue was as long as his entire body, and if an insect landed any where near him, the bug was an instant snack. Georgie lived on our lanai but often slipped through the sliding glass doors to find out what type of tasty insects might be inside. He was great entertainment just watching him skedaddle across the walls and ceiling on his daily hunts. He found cockroaches to be a challenge and one of his favorite meals.

Saipan sits dead center in the path of the Pacific typhoons which eventually end up in Taiwan or the Philippines. When Typhoon Kimster hit in September, we had to board up all the windows and make the hotel safe and secure. Naturally the children were worried about their adopted pets. Fur Ball ran off into the jungle, probably to find her own hole and a snuggly place to sit out the storm. Bruno came wandering over in the middle of the rain, looking for Annie. He was drenched and looking very weary and frightened. She had a found a safe place for him in the laundry room which would be secure with its concrete walls and roof. She fixed him up with food and water.

I suppose Scratchy headed to his home, wherever that was. We never saw him again until after the storm had subsided. Georgie just disappeared into the cracks in the wall or somewhere inside the furniture. Even in the middle of the storm, we saw him pop out several times on the walls with his head jerking up and down, still looking for another meal. Of course, the insects had already taken cover.

Three days later, it was clean-up time from the aftermath of the typhoon. There were palm fronds and corrugated tin roofs and other house parts from over the neighborhood in our swimming pool, on the beach, and in Yoshi's orchid garden. Coconuts were everywhere and had smashed the windows of a dozen cars. With new fittings and just a few adjustments, Mario II and his maintenance crew got the power and water working again. About an hour into the clean-up, Mario II came over to talk to Annie. He was very sad. Sometime during the storm, maybe the laundry door flew open during a strong wind gust or someone forgot to close up, but it appeared Bruno had slipped out during the worst part of the storm with winds climbing over 100 MPH and he hadn't been able to get back inside. The brave little mutt had died while trying to dig a hole for shelter under the hotel restaurant.

I was proud of Annie. She took it well, and the children dug a grave for him at jungle's edge on the eastside of the hotel. Annie built and painted a cross. As the family gathered, Annie said a few words about Bruno being a good friend, and lowered him into the hole wrapped in one of her favorite blankets. Fur Ball showed up during the memorial service, meowing for some lunch. She didn't seem particularly heart-broken about the loss of Bruno.

Food was scarce in the stores and would be until the supply ships managed to get ashore. That was bad news for Scratchy. We saw two local boys chasing him later in the afternoon. In the evening, we smelled a barbeque cooking away at our neighbor's home. Sure enough, when Anthony talked to the boys next day, Scratchy had been the special main course of the day. The boys said that they had been raising him and feeding him steroids to toughen him up and make him larger for the cock fighting arena; but that idea was soon forgotten when the family needed something to eat. The boys didn't mention any strange tastes or reactions to the steroids.

We have no idea what happened to Georgie – he was just gone one day.  Two other medium sized geckos moved into his territory, maybe his offspring.  It was interesting to watch nature take its course, as they barked at each other, did their challenging struts and push-ups, and then managed to have a fast-moving wrestling match on the walls.  Two days later, one of the lizards prevailed and now it was his territory.  Again, we haven't a clue what happened to his opponent.

Anthony and Annie's interests moved on.  Anthony got into baseball and football, with a little schooling and a lot of video games in between.  Annie loved clothes and make-up, and started noticing boys with a new intensity and, of course, vice-versa.

Donna and Fur Ball are still united.  That independent cat is still demanding her food on time, and if Donna is late, we get a bellyful of whining and screeching that can be heard all over the hotel.  Several tourists have been heard to say, "That poor cat…someone should find her something to eat."  When they approached to pet her, they'd back off real fast as her back arched and she did her hissing routine.  She didn't give a hoot about public relations, but she definitely had learned to control Donna.

# 4

## THE FUN-LOVING WAYWARD MANAGER

As Carlos and I returned from one of our hiking treks across the island, there was a message at the front desk to meet Cocina and Myla in the restaurant. Guangman knew that Carlos and I were in a 'slimming contest," so he had prepared a plate of fresh fruit and no-sugar ice tea – and no pastries.

We met the ladies in the back corner and knew we were in for a session of *tsismis,* the local gossip mill. I recognized their conspiratorial body language and they were both grinning. Being the front desk supervisor, Myla was usually privy to all the rumors and idle chatter on the island.

Cocina said, "It finally happened. I knew Joi Young at the Golden Executive Hotel wouldn't last. He was too much of a party-animal."

Myla added, "His reputation is terrible. We get some of the guests that started in his hotel and then transfer over here after bad service and noisy parties."

Basically anyone on Saipan in the hospitality industry knew that Joi was on a downward slide. He got the top rate hotel on Saipan after a successful business career. Joi knew it was a golf mecca and a plum assignment that was busy and profitable but not overflowing with guests and problems. He had served his company for over thirty years and had reached the top rung of his career after working long hours with little vacation time.

Unfortunately along the way, Joi had developed some bad habits such as smoking, drinking, a little gambling, and too many ladies. He was married but that had not stopped his womanizing. After visiting Saipan a few times, his wife Cho got homesick and decided to stay in Korea with their grandchildren. This was not good for Joi and his worsening habits. She was the control factor in his life, which of course, helped him stay straight and concentrate on the hotel and his job.

Joi arrived on Saipan with a great deal of fanfare from the local government, and special welcoming from his managers, as well as the owners and directors from the other hotels. That's how Cocina and I met him, and also Cho. Cocina and Cho became good friends. Joi got off to a flying start and he was productive and proactive, and his staff very supportive. With Cho back home, foolishly Joi started drinking heavily with his guests and soon, playing the big shot, he was giving away too many drinks and expensive food. He also started showing up for work later and later, causing others to do his work and covering for him, and worse of all, not sending his monthly reports back to Seoul on time. He received several negative phone calls and emails from the home office.

All this consternation caused additional stress and resulted in him drinking more and every night. He also made ventures to Tinian to the gambling casinos with his new- found, freeloading entourage. The losses were mounting up and later the hotel auditors found that he charged much of his losses to the company credit cards. But more than all these transgressions, he demoralized his entire staff when he started bringing prostitutes to his hotel apartment. The security crew had been trying to keep the girls out of the hotel rooms, while on the other hand, the big boss was bringing them in. The prosties liked it because he gave big tips, and also allowed them to visit their friends and meet new clients. The girls started cruising the front of the hotel, hoping for a profitable session, sometimes approaching a man with his wife alongside.

A whistleblower sent complaints to the home office in Japan. The home bosses had already heard some rumblings and were concerned about the diminishing profit margin. The hotel chain had an inspection team that went from property to property and ironically for two years,

Joi had been a member of a previous team. Off the team went to Saipan and made contact with the whistleblower.

The inspection team stayed at our hotel through secret arrangements with Cocina. Right after dinner, the team made a surprise visit to Joi's hotel. He was not in his office and no one knew where he was. He didn't answer his cell or apartment phone. The security supervisor took the inspectors to his room and after knocking and the door opening, they were greeted with loud music with people laughing and carousing. Many of the party-goers appeared to be street ladies, and they found Joi in the kitchen with his shirt off, wearing only his shorts. He had a prostitute on his lap and was drinking very expensive hotel scotch whiskey. He was drunk and beyond understanding the seriousness of the situation. He slapped one of the inspectors on the back and invited him to have a drink.

The inspectors sent everyone home and told Joi to report to his office in the morning. They took numerous photographs. Adding to his stupidity, Joi said to the team supervisor, "C'mon Chong. Let's drink and forget all these regulations. Let's have fun. I can get you a nice Chinese girl." As the exiting crew slammed the door, he was left talking to himself.

The hotel inspection team had authority to make significant decisions on the spot. They spoke to Joi in the morning to get his version of the party and the declining profit. He was hung-over, speechless and embarrassed after being caught red-handed. The team supervisor decided that Joi's retirement was in order.

I asked, "Did they treat him with respect after all those years?"

Cocina said, "After he was relieved by the team, he went home on the next plane. He had only lasted for fourteen months on Saipan. The company gave him a large retirement party with certificates, new golf clubs and a gold watch. He didn't lose face. His wife Cho had him lined up for substance abuse and sexual addiction counseling the next day."

I said, "Probably be tough for him to break his old habits, but if he can, he'll end his years living quietly as an attentive grandfather to the children. Every time there's another hotel retirement party, he'll get his invitation, and he can travel and visit the other hotels gratis."

"Oh, don't worry. He'll make it or find himself out on the streets. I know Cho – she's a tough old gal."

"Shape up, or ship out eh?"

"Same goes for you, Buster. Don't ever screw around on your sweetie. You might be disciplined."

"My room, or your room?"

"Our room, you Big Dope…"

# 5

# COCINA'S EMAILS

Always moving forward, part of Cocina's Americanization was her discovery of email and the funny stories that circulated. She sincerely enjoyed her computer and the link to the outside world. She didn't quite understand the mainland's sense of humor, some of the colloquialisms, subtleties, and innuendos in language, so she often brought them to me for interpretation, but only after a gaggle of Filipinas had tried to sort them out. It's true that when a group or committee tries to describe a giraffe, the final product often appears more like a hippopotamus. Her little cluster of interpreters often made her more confused. Being my first language, I speak and understand a passable amount of the English language but still had trouble figuring out the emails at times. I can well imagine the challenge of interpreting some of the messages if English was my second language. These are some of her favorites, open to anyone's interpretation.

Some of emails have been circulating for many years, but they were new for Cocina and her friends.

\*    \*    \*

### The World's Shortest Fairy Tale

Once upon a time, a girl asked a guy, "Will you marry me?" The guy said, "No." And the girl lived happily ever after. She went shopping, drank pina coladas with friends, always had a clean house, never had to cook, had a closet full of shoes and handbags, stayed skinny and was never farted on. The End.

### An Oldie but Goodie – A Dirty Joke

A woman getting married for the fourth time goes to a bridal shop and asks for a white dress from the sales clerk. Puzzled, the sales clerk says, "You've been married three times already. A white dress doesn't seem right." "Of course, I can wear a white dress. I'm still a virgin."
"Impossible," replies the sales clerk.
"Unfortunately not," the bride explained. "My first husband was a psychologist. All he did was talk about it. My second husband was a gynecologist. All he wanted to do was look at it. My third husband was a stamp collector. Gosh-almighty, I really miss him!"

### Blonde at the River

Joanne, a blonde, is out for walk. She comes to a river and sees another blonde, Trish, on the opposite bank. "Yoo-hoo!" Joanne shouts, and "How can I get to the other side?" Trish looks up the river, then down the river and shouts back, "You are on the other side!"

### The Blonde and a Vacuum

A blonde was splaying Trivial Pursuit one night. It was her turn. She rolled the dice and landed on Science and Nature. Her question was, "If you are in a vacuum and someone calls your name, can you hear it?" She thought for a moment and then asked, "Is the vacuum off or on?"

### The Blonde's Fatal Attraction

A blonde who suspects her boyfriend of cheating goes out and buys a gun. She goes to his apartment unexpectedly, opens the door with her key, and sure enough, finds him naked in the arms of a luscious brunette. She's totally angry. She opens her purse and takes out the gun. But as she does so, she is overcome with grief and points the gun at her own head. The boyfriend exclaims, "No, Honey, don't do it." "Shut up," she yells, "You're next!"

### The Irish Blonde

An attractive, full-breasted blonde from Cork, Ireland arrived at the casino. She seemed a little intoxicated and bet 20,000 Euros on a single roll of the dice. She said, "I hope you don't mind, but I feel luckier when I'm completely nude."

With that, she stripped from the neck down, rolled the dice, and with a noticeable Irish brogue, yelled, "Come on, baby, Mama needs new clothes!" As the dice came to a stop, she jumped up and down and squealed, "Yes! Yes! I won! I won!"

She hugged each of the dealers and then picked up her winnings and her clothes, and quickly departed. The dealers stared at each other, dumbfounded. Finally, one of the dealers asked, "What did she roll?" The other one answered, "I don't know. I thought you were watching."

Moral of the Story: Not all Irish are drinkers, not all blondes are dumb, but all men…are men!

### The Meaning of Names

A woman arrived at a party and while scanning the guests, spotted an attractive man standing alone. She approached him, smiled and said, "Hello, my name is Carmen." He replied, "That's a beautiful name. Is it a family name?"

"Actually I gave it to myself. It represents the things that I enjoy the most – cars and men. Therefore, I chose Carmen. What's your name?"

He answered, "B.J. Titsangolf."

### Weak Soldier

Impotence is just Nature's Way of saying "No Hard Feelings."

### Soothing Assistance on the Golf Course

Two women are playing golf on a sunny afternoon when one of them accidentally slices her shot into a foursome of men. To her horror, one of the men collapses in agony, both hands in his crotch area. She runs down to him, apologizing profusely, explaining that she is a physical therapist and can help ease his pain. "No, thanks…just give me a few minutes…I'll be fine," he replies quietly, hands held between his legs. Taking it upon herself to help the poor man, she gently undoes the front of his pants and starts massaging his genitals. "Doesn't that feel better?" she asks. "Well, yes…that's pretty good," then admits, "But my thumb still hurts like hell."

## English Is Important
From a fun Canadian: "I had a bunch of American dollars to exchange, so I went to the currency exchange window at a local bank. Short line, no problem.  Just one lady was in front of me…an Asian lady who was trying to exchange yen for dollars, and she was a little irritated.
She asked the teller, "Why it change? Yesterday, I get two hunat dolla for yen. Toy, I get hunat eighty."
The teller shrugged her shoulders and said, "Fluctuations."
The Asian lady asserted, "Fuc you white people too!"

## Medical  Communication
Arlene, a nurse making her rounds: A white patient asked her, "Are my testicles black?"  Arlene replied, "What? No, your testicles are not black." The patient asked again, "Please, are my testicles black?" Arlene answered, "My dear, trust me.  Your testicles are not black."  For the third time, the patient asked again, "Are my testicles black?"
"Ok, then. I'll check."  She dutifully lifted the blanket and looked into the patient's private parts, held each one in her hand, and even turned his penis left to right. She asserted, "Nope, your testicles are not black.  Satisfied?"
The patient then removed the oxygen mask from his face, unmuffling his speech and stated, "I said, are test results back yet?"

## Life
Life isn't like a bowl of cherries and peaches, It's more like as jar of jalapenos. What you do today, might burn your ass tomorrow."

## Priorities
An old lady is standing at the rail of a cruise ship holding her hat so it wouldn't blow away in the wind.

A gentleman approached her and said, "Pardon me, Madam. I do not intend to be forward but did you know your dress is blowing up in the wind?"

"Yes, I know," said the lady. "But I need my hands to hold onto my hat."

"But Madam," he said, "You must know that your derriere is exposed."

The woman looked down, then back up at the man and said, "Sir, anything you can see down there is over 75 years old…but I just bought this hat yesterday!"

Husband Down

A husband and wife were shopping in their local mega-department store. The husband picks up a case of beer and puts it in the cart. The wife asks, "What do you think you're doing. He answers, "They're on sale, only $10 for 24 cans." She demands, "Put them back, we can't afford them."

They carry on shopping and a few aisles down, the wife picks up a $20 jar of face cream and puts it in the basket. "What do you think you're doing?" asks the husband. She replies, "It's my favorite face cream. It makes me look beautiful." The husband stupidly retorts, "So does 24 cans of beer and it's half the price!"

Over the store PA System: "Clean-up needed on cosmetics aisle. We have a husband down."

Sunday Morning Sex

I will never hear church bells ringing without smiling…Upon learning that her elderly grandfather has just passed away, Judy went straight to her grandparents' house to visit her 96-year-old grandmother and comfort her.

When Judy asked how her grandfather had died, her grandmother replied, "He had a heart attack while we were making love on Sunday morning." Horrified, Judy told her grandmother that two people nearly 100 years old having sex would surely be asking for trouble. "Oh no, my dear, " replied granny. "Many years ago, realizing our advanced age, we figured out the best time to do it was when the church bells would start

to ring. It was just the right rhythm. Nice and slow and even. Nothing too strenuous, simply in on the <u>ding</u> and out on the <u>dong</u>."
She paused to wipe away a tear and continued, "He'd still be alive if the damn ice cream truck hadn't come along."

## Listen and Learn

A very short story: Man driving down the road. Woman driving up same road. They pass each other. The woman yells out the window, "Pig!" The man yells back out his window, "Bitch!" Man rounds next corner and crashes into a huge pig in the middle of the road and dies. If only men would listen…

## Health Plans

A wealthy hospital benefactor was being shown the hospital by Dr. Ramirez and Dr. Carter. During her tour she passed a room where a male patient was masturbating furiously. "Oh my gawd!" screamed the woman, "That's disgraceful! Why is he doing that?" Dr. Ramirez, who was leading the tour calmly explained, "I'm very sorry that you were exposed to that but this man has a serious condition where his testicles rapidly fill with semen and if he doesn't do that at least five times a day, he'll be in extreme pain and his testicles could easily rupture."
"Oh well, in that case, I guess it's okay," commented the woman. In the very next room, a male patient was lying in bed and it was obvious that a nurse was performing oral sex on him. Again, the woman screamed, "Oh my gawd. How can that be justified?" This time, Dr. Carter spoke very calmly and said, "Same illness, better health plan."

## Cowboy Rodeo Humor

Two Oklahoma cowboys were out on the range talking about their favorite sex positions. One said, "I think I enjoy the rodeo position the best." "I don't think I've ever heard of that one," said the other cowboy, "What is it?"
"Well, it's where you got your wife down on all fours and you mount her from behind. Then you reach down and cup each one of her breasts and whisper in her ear, 'Wowee, these feel just like your sister's.' Then you try and stay on for eight seconds."

## The Cowboy Entrepreneur

Young George in Idaho bought a horse from a farmer for $100. The farmer agreed to deliver the horse on the morrow. The next day he drove up and said, "Sorry son, but I have some bad news. The horse died." George replied, "Well, then just give me back my money and we'll be square."

The farmer said, "I can't do that. I went and spent it already. George said, "OK then, just bring me the dead horse."

The farmer asked, 'What are you going to do with him?" George said, "I'll going to raffle him off." The farmer declared, "You can't raffle off a dead horse." George said, "Sure I can. Watch me. I just won't tell anyone that he'd dead."

A month later, the farmer met up with young George and asked, "What happened with that dead horse?" George said, "I raffled him off. I sold 500 tickets at $2 a piece and made a profit of $998." The farmer queried, "Didn't anyone complain?"

George said, "Just the cowboy that won. So I gave him back his $2."

George grew up and now works for the federal government. He was the one that figured how to bail us out in the auto industry and the banks!

## Management Notice

"This Department requires no physical fitness program. Everyone gets enough exercise jumping to conclusions, flying off the handle, running down the boss, knifing friends in the back, dodging responsibility and pushing their luck…"

## Management Thought for the Day

Life at work is like a tree full of monkeys, all on different limbs at different levels. Some monkeys are climbing up, some down; the monkeys on top look down and see a tree full of smiling faces. The monkeys on the bottom look up and see nothing but assholes.

## Business Proposal

Jorge wanted to have sex with a girl in his office, but she said she already had a boyfriend. One day he got so horny and frustrated that he went up to her and said, "I'll give you a $100 if you let me have sex with you."

The girl said, "No!" Then Jorge said, "I'll be fast. I'll throw the money on the floor, you bend down and I'll be finished by the time you pick it up." She thought for a moment and said she would have to consult her boyfriend and told him the story. The boyfriend said, "Ask him for $200 and pick up the money real fast. He won't even be able to get his pants down." She agreed and accepted the proposal. A half hour went by. Finally, after 45 minutes the boyfriend called and asked what happened. She said, "The bastard used quarters!" Management lesson: Always consider a business proposal in it entirety before agreeing to it and getting screwed.

Go Fly a Kite

A husband is in his backyard trying to fly a kite. He throws the kite up, the wind catches it for a few seconds and then it come crashing back down. He tried this a few more times with no success. All the time his wife is watching him from the kitchen window, muttering to herself how men need to be told how to do everything. She opens the window and yells to her husband, "You need a piece of tail." The man turned around with a confused look on his face and said, "Make up your mind. Last night you told me to go fly a kite."

Onions and Christmas Trees

A family is at the dinner table. The son asks his father, "Dad, how many kinds of boobs are there?" The surprised father answers, "Well, Son, there are three kinds of boobs. In her 20's, a woman's are like melons, round and firm; in her 30's and 40's, they're like pears, still nice but hanging a bit. After 50, they're like onions."
"Onions?"
"Yes, you see them and they make you cry."
This infuriates his wife and daughter, so the daughter asks, "Mom, how many kinds of "willies" are there?" The surprised mother answers, "Well Dear, a man goes through three phases. In his 20's, his willy is like an oak tree, mighty and hard; in his 30's and 40's, it's like a birch, flexible but reliable. After his 50's, it's like a Christmas tree."
"A Christmas tree?"
"Yes, Dear, the root's dead and the balls are just for decoration."

## Ladies of the Night Emails…

Union:
A dedicated Teamsters Union worker was attending a convention in Las Vegas and, as you might expect, decided to check out the brothels nearby. When he got to the first one, he asked the Madame, "Is this a union house?" "No," she replied, "I'm sorry it isn't." "Well, if I pay you $100, what cut do the girls get?" "The house get $80 and the girls get $20." Mightily offended by such unfair dealings, the man stomped off down the street in search of a more equitable, hopefully unionized shop. His search continued until he finally reached a brothel where the Madame responded, "Why, yes sir, this is a union house." The man asked, "And if pay you $100, what cut do the girls get?" "The girls get $80 and the house gets $20." That's more like it!" the union man said. He handed the Madame $100, looked around the room and pointed to a stunningly attractive brunette. "I'd like her for the night." "I'm sure you would, sir," said the Madame, then gesturing to an 85-year-old woman in the corner, "but according to the union rules, Edith here has seniority."

Tough Prostitute:
One day after striking gold in Alaska, a lonesome miner came down from the mountains and walked into a saloon in the nearest town. "I'm looking for the meanest, toughest, and roughest hooker in the Yukon," he said to the bartender. "We've got her," replied the bartender, "She's upstairs in the second room on the right." The miner handed the bartender a gold nugget to pay for the hooker and two beers. He grabbed the bottles, ran up the stairs, kicked the door open on the right and yelled, "I'm looking for the meanest, roughest and toughest hooker in the Yukon." The woman inside the room looked at the miner, stripped down, and grabbed her ankles. "How do you know I want that position right away?" asked the miner. "I don't," replied the hooker, "but I thought you might wanna open those beers first."

Surprise!
A guy is walking along the strip in Las Vegas and a knockout hooker catches his eyes. He strikes up a conversation so he eventually says,

"How much?" "It starts at $500 for a hand-job." The man says, "$500 for a hand-job. No hand-job is worth that much money." The hooker replies, "Do you see the Irish Bar on the corner?" "Yes." "Do you see the Irish Bar about a block further down?" "Yes." "And beyond that, do you see the third Irish bar?" "Yes." "Well," says the hooker, ""I own those. And I own them because I give a hand-job that worth $500." The guy says, "What the hell. I'll give it a try." They retired to a nearby motel.

A short time later, the guys is sitting on the bed realizing that he had just experienced the hand-job of a lifetime, worth every bit of $500. He is so amazed, he says, "I suppose a blow-job is $1000?" The hooker replies, "$1500." The guys says, "$1500? No blow-job can be worth that much." The hooker replies, "Step over her to the window, Big Boy. Do you see that casino just across the street? I own that casino outright. And I own it because I give a blow-job that worth every cent of $1500." The guy, basking in the afterglow of the terrific hand-job, says, "Sign me up."

Ten  minutes later, he is sitting on the bed more amazed that before. He can scarcely believe it but he feels he truly got his money's worth. He decides to dip into the retirement savings for one more glorious and unforgettable experience. He asked the hooker, "How much for pussy?" The hooker says, "Come over here to the window  Do you see the whole city of Las Vegas is laid out before us, those beautiful lights, gambling palaces, and showplaces?" "Damn," the guy says in awe, "You own the whole city?" "No" the hooker replied, "but I would if I had a pussy."

## Golfing and Hooking

A man and woman meet on vacation, get busy and quickly fall in love. At the trip's end, they decide to open up to each other. It's only fair to warn you, Isabel," Bob says, "I'm a golf nut. I live, eat, sleep, and breathe golf."

"Well, I'll be honest, too," Isabel says, "I'm a hooker."

The man looked crestfallen for a moment, then asks, "Are you keeping your wrists straight?"

\*        \*        \*

Needless to say, it was merriment and laughter whenever Cocina opened her emails. We've all seen the blank expressions when people don't get the moral or the meaning of a joke, and then an hour later, you hear them busting up. Sometimes the laughter with Cocina and her friends didn't break loose until the next day and you were liable to hear uproarious chatter, followed by a flurry of texts and cell phone calls to one another. This was learning conversational English at its best... with tons of chuckles and laughter making the day a little easier and a lot more fun.

I still a hard time on some of them getting the gist of the joke or story. I knew Cocina was getting Americanized when she was able to explain several of the tough ones. I loved it when she used the term "punch line" about the email.

Cocina never did quite understand why blondes were often the brunt of the stories.

# 6

## I'M RUBBIN' IT!

Carlos and I were kicking back in the Private Investigations Office waiting for the coffee to brew. No word on the missing governor and the contract. Guangman had dropped off some fresh baked croissants from the hotel restaurant, and there was no way ex- cops could eat pastries without some fresh Kona coffee. With the coffee perking, our little office smelled like a downtown California Starbuck's. Very nice aroma. We had nothing planned – just a few legal papers to serve to elusive recipients and dead-beat dads. The phone rang.

Carlos picked up and I saw him nodding and smiling. He kept saying, "Yep, sure thing. Yeah, right. You're sure?" He concluded, "Yep, we're on the way."

Carlos grabbed his camera and note pad, and said, "We gotta rock and roll. Some Japanese guys are filming a porno down at McClucky's Chicken House, and the boss doesn't want the media involved." The fast food restaurant was owned by an older, conservative, church-going, Bible-thumping geezer named Januario "Janny" Muleta. Carlos said that Janny was really ticked off when the crew told him to wait a few minutes before they stopped filming. On the way, Janny called again, and held the phone over the shielding blanket near the lovemaking. He said, "Does that sound like a girl climaxing or what?" It was a very nice, satisfying, but stifled scream.

Carlos said, "I wonder if she looks as good as she sounds?"

I summarized, "This could definitely be interesting."

We arrived in less than ten minutes. The camera crew members were packing up their cameras, and other workers were taking down a blanket that had been set up to hide the actors. A young Japanese lady was adjusting her skirt, and an older, handsome man was buckling up his trousers. There was a red matching panty and bra set still under the dining table. I saw Janny yelling at a grizzled, pony tailed Japanese man, who appeared to be in charge of the operation.

Carlos and I introduced ourselves to the Japanese man. His name was Yuki Ishii and he was the producer and director of the operation. He said that he was filming a sex movie with a theme that a lusty young girl wants to make love in all her favorite places. She also allegedly liked mature, experienced men as lovers. They had already filmed at a beach and the airport. They still intended to film a sequence at the movie theatre and a billiard parlor. I told him to get everyone's ID and passports, and that we would talk to them in a few minutes.

I spoke to Janny out front, along with several patrons, who said that the director and the fully-clothed actors had filmed outside the restaurant, then had come in, ordered some food, then moved to a corner area not easily visible to other customers. They were suspicious-looking because the girl was gorgeous and at best, the men were average-looking guys. Janny said that he became really curious when they put up some blankets for privacy shields and started the cameras rolling. He heard some noises behind the blanket that sounded like sexual pleasure. The lady seemed to be moaning. When he looked over the blanket, the man had his hand up the lady's skirt and was pulling down her panties. She was already bare-breasted, and the man was holding her bra in his teeth. She was holding the man's erect penis with her hands and rubbing the tip.

Janny added, "That's when I called you guys. They wouldn't stop when I told them to get out. The director's response was 'You're ruining the sound. Now shut up!' So, I screamed at them some more." He paused, "I just don't want bad publicity. If the word got out at church that a porno was being shot at my restaurant, it would ruin my reputation. You know island gossip."

Carlos said, "We'll talk to them and get all the details, and then get them out of here. You're still sure about 'no cops?' It's easy to haul them away for indecent behavior in public." Janny shook his head.

Wise-cracking, fun-loving Carlos couldn't help himself when he said, "Or pubic in public." Janny wasn't amused. I was though and had to fight back a grin.

We sat at a booth with the director and had all the actors and crew members come over one at a time. I noticed that the bra and panties had been picked up and that the lead actress had ducked into the rest room. Each of the workers came by with valid identification and passports. Most of them spoke passable English.

The twenty-two-year-old actress, Masako Shimada, was a beautiful young woman and a dental nurse by occupation. She was obviously intelligent and a college graduate. She only worked part-time as a porn star to earn some cash for her boyfriend's new car and for their honeymoon in Hawaii. It was an old familiar story. The boyfriend was "temporarily unemployed and planning to go back to college after their wedding." She said, "Right now, we need the money. I'll stop doing porn after he gets a job."

Carlos asked, "Aren't you afraid of being recognized by someone in your family or maybe your friends?"

She answered, "First they would have to admit that they were watching pornography, and then for each shoot, I change my hair style, use lots of make-up and wear sexy clothes. Back home, I wear very conservative clothes and no make-up. It's an old joke, but many of us do look alike – all from the same gene pool. If someone would say anything to me about it, I'll just say it wasn't me. Even my boyfriend thinks I'm off on a dental convention with my doctor friends."

The lead male star, Makota Ochai, was hired just for two scenes. Because the female protagonist was supposedly seeking out new men at the different locations, he was scheduled for the McClucky's scene. He had already finished the one at the airport in semi-darkness and wouldn't be recognized as the same guy in both sequences. Makota was the new breed of porn star in Japan. A whole new billion-dollar industry had developed in "senior porn" for a country that was becoming sexless until the porn industry marketed the senior citizens. Stars like 73-year-old Makota were in demand with themes like teaching young girls about sex, or seducing mature actresses who had been living without sex and were suddenly full of juice and desire. He was due to go back to Japan next morning to shoot two more films. Japan's largest video-store chain Tsutaya, was introducing about one thousand new adult titles per month.

The man in the earlier beach scene, Gaichi Takuda, happened to be a performer from a visiting Japanese dance troupe and being single, wasn't worried about being recognized and was more than happy to hump Masako in the warm ocean water. He didn't charge Yuki for his services. Instead he invited Masako to dinner and an all-expenses-paid night in his room. Masako enjoyed her work.

Yuki explained that the X-rated production companies were using more outside or free locations to cut costs. He said, "Ten years ago, we could do a cheap adult film for about one million yen. Now we only get about five hundred thousand yen, and sometimes even lower. There is so much competition. Those rates give you no leeway to book a studio or a nice hotel room, rent extra equipment and pay wages. Most adult movie actresses are the highest paid workers in each flick. But new girls like Masako get only about seventy thousand yen and the guys get far less. Patrons like to see new girls and most of our new girls are nurses like Masako, aspiring actresses, bored housewives and a lot of military women. Mature women are really in vogue. Female soldiers are very popular in the army for obvious reasons, and they fuck a lot of fellow soldiers for free, so they figure they might as well be paid for their lovemaking."

I asked, "So that's why you pick a public place like McClucky's? No rental costs but it doesn't seem be worth the risk of being arrested."

Yuki answered, "So we get busted and end up with pages of free publicity about the flick."

"What now?" asked Carlos.

"Glad you asked."  He said to Carlos, "I've already chatted with Masako. We could change the theme of the movie a bit, and besides making love in favorite locations, we could add lovers of different racial make-up. When I mentioned you, she said, "He's so chestnut-brown and handsome; I'm getting wetter and wetter just thinking about him on top of me.' So how about it? She's ready right now. Maybe on a cool mountain top overlooking the lagoon…"

Carlos got a silly grin and asked, "How about Tom? Does she want a big, tough white guy?"

"She already agreed to Tom. She's a little worried because she's heard that white guys have huge cocks."

I said, "Not to worry in that area. She'll get a good giggle. But there's a few other problems like it's against the law for sexual intercourse in public, and also our wives own machetes."

Yuki exclaimed, "Not good! Ouch! I didn't know you fellows were married."

I replied, "Yep, we are. So you'll have to find some other actors for your next scene. Besides, how do those studs get it up with all the people and cameras everywhere?"

Yuki laughed, "I've often wonder about that myself. They must be horny bastards or use a lot of blue pills." He paused and looked at Carlos. "I didn't hear you object to the starring role."

Carlos said, "The only difference between our wives is that my wife's machete is dull and rusty."

Yuki said, "Oh, double ouch!"

Because of the business folks that we knew, and because the movie company was producing a movie that people wanted, Carlos and I arranged for the production company to use the movie theatre after hours, and also a pool hall. The two new Japanese lovers came in from Japan on schedule, and after a few wines, Masako liked them both, at least enough for a sensuous session with one of the men, and the last man, a body-builder, for the three-hole finale in the pool hall.

I was invited to the last session. There were about ten people watching the scene. The man developed a massive erection on cue. Masako became a mad demon when he entered her anally. She screamed in ecstasy and her little body quivered in climax, all the time massaging her clitoris with her right hand. She was covered in sweat and her eyes were glazed over. She sighed one last time and went limp.

Always wondering about different life styles, Cocina had asked to meet Masako. After her last session and a quick shower, Masako came with me to our hotel. Cocina gave her a wonderful Japanese *Yokoso!* welcome with flowers and sweet wine. She planned to rest up before her trip home to Japan and Cocina had arranged for a nice quiet room. I sat with the ladies and listened as they talked about clothes and shoes, travel and future plans. No one would have ever known that Masako had been humping and bumping across three different pool tables just a few hours before.

I always admire the joy and mystery of women – and their survival strengths.

Three weeks later, I received a call from Yuki. He said that he was scouting a new location to shoot three to four adult films. Makota Ochai was coming back with several older ladies in his movie harem. The scenery, weather, and photography from Saipan had turned out perfectly. He asked if I had any ideas about a good location. He was hinting at using my hotel but that was never going to happen. Naked people would cause too many heart attacks among my fuddy-duddy senior citizen clientele.

Jokingly, he said, "Maybe we could have a special showing for the seniors in your conference room…or better yet, find some new amateur actors for my films. You know the audiences love to see the old people getting it on."

I checked with a real estate friend and found him an empty spartan hotel, high on a bluff with a magnificent view of the harbor. It had its own swimming pool with an underground bar with a viewing area of the swimmers and plenty of privacy from the neighbors. I figured that looking at naked swimmers from a below window would make some interesting filming for sure. The paperwork was completed and Yuki planned to bring his whole crew back again, including little Masako for another "dental conference."

# 7

# DON'T BE SO ROUGH

When the people of the Northern Mariana Islands became American citizens, they were able to travel freely to the mainland, and elsewhere, carrying the blue US passport. The young people were urgently needed during the wars in Iraq and Afghanistan, and they signed up for the adventure and educational benefits and to get off the small islands for career and travel opportunities. Per capita, the Pacific islands have the highest enlistment and casualty rate in the entire US military services.

Mario I, our hotel accountant, told me a family story one night around the beach campfire. Apparently his daughter, Julie, got into a little trouble in the Army but proudly he said, "The girl stood her ground like her mother and I always taught her.

As a new recruit, Julie did her basic training at Fort Jackson, South Carolina. Islanders had never been exposed to blatant racism, except what they saw in a movie or on TV. Micronesians are a mixture of former sailors, Japanese soldiers, Chinese merchants, pirates, Spanish colonists, rogues who ran away from regular society anywhere in the world, and then from the USA since 1946. They are a blend of many races, languages and cultures, and not generally inclined to discrimination or bias.

Julie had top scores in ROTC and was a member of the honor society for three straight years in high school. She was excited about her US Army Boot Camp, a regular paycheck, and the educational opportunity to work later for a law degree. She was assigned to a barracks with about sixty other women, with an almost equal one-third ratio of Caucasian, Hispanic and African Americans. She was the only islander. To her dismay, there seemed to be friction between the Caucasian and African-Americans groups. The Hispanics stayed out it, and they weren't pressured about anything. The informal leader of the African-Americans, Georgia, tried to get Julie to side with them against the Caucasians for the control of the barracks. Control meant who would use the bathroom first, go to chow first, and who would do the cleaning in the barracks. Julie was surprised to see that some of the Caucasian women were frightened and followed orders from Georgia and her group. She saw several of them crying themselves to sleep every night.

Julie declined the offer to join with Georgia and said that she would not side with anyone. Her goal was to finish the training, complete soldierization (as the drill instructors called making one into a soldier), and get on with her career plans. Georgia threatened Julie with an "ass-kicking" in front of ten other women, adding that she would regret her decision. Julie brushed her aside and said, "You do what you have to do."

The next day the ladies had one-on-one fighting with long padded sticks called "pugles." Most Americans, especially females, have never thrown a punch in anger, or been in a fight, or been trained to kill when necessary. This training is part of the soldierization process. Recruits learn how to fight and to protect themselves. As fate would have it, Georgia and Julie were paired off in the same pit for fighting. Georgia got off a major hit on Julie, and asserted, "This is only the beginning, you Bitch!"

Julie didn't noticeably react and took another hit. She calmly said, "So be it. You called it." Georgia had no idea that Julie had been a baseball and basketball player and had been in many fights during the athletic contests. She also had a tough-girl reputation back home after breaking a girl's jaw in a fight over a boyfriend.

In the pit, Julie's response was swift and direct. Georgia took a hit on her head, followed by a straight-on blow to the frontal neck area. She went down, and started grimacing in pain. Julie followed her down, with full intention of finishing her with another shot. The drill instructors jumped into the pit and pulled Julie off. The medics were called, and Georgia was hauled off to the base hospital. After x-rays were taken, it was determined that Georgia's collar bone was broken. She had to be recycled into another training session.

Julie was called into the Captain's office. When she saw that the captain was an African-American, her alarm circuits went off full throttle. He questioned her about the conflict and she was honest and straightforward. He had the drill instructors' reports in front of him. He treated her fairly, and simply advised her "not to be so rough next time." Following the required salute, she noticed that the captain was grinning.

After the confrontation in the pit, and some intervention from the training staff, the barracks calmed down, and the women went on to a successful graduation. It made Julie feel fully accepted and welcome, when she was hugged by Caucasian and African- Americans graduates alike, and even better, when she saw them hugging each other. The Hispanics hugged one and all, simply saying, "Bueno. Bring on the advanced training classes."

Julie smiled to herself while getting ready for her next assignment, knowing that the army recognizes only two colors – "camouflage green" or "camouflage tan."

I said, "Good story. No wonder you're proud of the girl."

"I love that girl and I really have fun telling the story. That woman Georgia had no concept of Julie's history. Julie knows. I told her all about her ancestors. Her great-great-great-great grandfather on my side was a black sailor on a merchant ship out of Massachusetts. We have a large family and there are literally hundreds of offspring carrying his blood."

"And all this time, I thought you were a thoroughbred."

"Yeah, right. How about you?"

"Let's see. Part Viking pillager, part Norman invader, part Roman conqueror and some Visigoth on my mother's side."

"Typical American eh." Mario I laughed.

"You got it...unfortunate that the bigots and religious coo-coos don't wise up."

# 8

## BIG DICK, THE DOG NAPPER

As Carlos liked to say, "We get the damnest cases, the ones that DPS can't handle or don't want to be bothered."

This one was no different. Our potential client was a business man named Joon Ko Jung, who was complaining that a dog salesman was selling him meat full of chemicals and his customers were complaining about the taste and the indigestion that followed. Several of the male customers said that they farted so loudly that their wives forced them to sleep outside on the lanai, and then in the morning, the neighbors commented about the stench and wanted to know if there was something dead in their rooms.

I explained that Saipan Public Health didn't allow the sale or consumption of dog meat. Joon played ignorant about the law. He said that specially-prepared dog is a popular dish in Korea, and that he's been buying dog and serving it surreptitiously for over five years. The men like to eat it along with drinking their Korean liquor *sogu*.

I knew right away that mainlanders took their well-fed dogs to the vet for their shots and vitamins and that a lot of the dogs had been come up missing, probably kidnapped and hauled away to butcher for the Korean restaurants. These dogs would be fat and healthy after being cared for as pets but not suitable for eating, being full of chemicals and medicines. It was no mystery why the meat would be hard to digest. It was like eating a handful of pills combined with alcohol.

Since the police couldn't very well handle the case because of the illegality of the complainant, we said we would help out but on the agreement that dog, or cat, would no longer be served in the restaurant. I asked him to convince the other Korean restaurant owners to do the same. Joon reluctantly agreed, knowing that fresh seafood was also popular and that the ocean was full of natural tasty morsels. Joon gave us the basic information about the salesman, Ricardo Reyes from the Village of San Roque.

Our intention was to contact Ricardo and tell him to stop stealing and processing dogs and cats for sales to the restaurants. After checking with a few of the villagers, especially the women that giggled when we mentioned Ricardo's name, they knew right away who we were talking about. He bought and sold dogs, but what was even more interesting and truly memorable, he had been servicing women for most of his adult life. Apparently his sexual appendage was something to be admired, at least by the ladies, and they had coined his *palayaw* - nickname "Big Dick."

The ladies were reluctant to tell us where he lived. Although a source of pleasure to the female gender, he was also a man that would give you a few bucks for a chubby dog and also helped in controlling the increasing number of feral boonie dogs. If village lads needed money for fuel, or for the movies, or for a new shirt, the lad could pick up some fast money for catching some dogs for butchering and selling them to Ricardo. Unfortunately, some of the household pets liked jumping into any vehicle for a ride, licking the kidnapper and jumping for joy, and ending up with Big Dick.

When Big Dick did his butchering, the wild meat and the pet meat often got mixed together, so he was never sure of what he was selling and to whom. We soon learned that he had no idea of how a pet dog was nutritiously and chemically different than a feral mutt. Organic and safe were not in his vocabulary. The local connoisseurs knew that *aso kalye* – street dog was the best for eating; and they all seemed to have a favorite recipe for cooking dog, stew being the favorite after marinating the meat in Seven-Up or Sprite.

Carlos talked to a dozen more people in the local language, and soon we found a middle-aged lady, Sophie, who had been dumped by Big Dick five years prior. It appeared that Big Dick dropped his love mates once they reached forty, and then would go after their daughters. Most recently he had moved in a Filipino about twenty-five-years-old and had already impregnated her twice. Sophie said, "He was not only a satisfier, but had strong seed." She figured that about a fourth of the children in the village could be traced back to Big Dick. She thought maybe some half-brothers and half-sisters ended up marrying each other, or at least having babies together. So far, there hadn't been a lot of birth defects with kids having three eyes or four arms.

Carlos asked her about the men in the village. She figured the men hadn't killed him because he was a source of income for the village and that he was generous in buying plenty of cold beer. It was evident that she held the islanders' casual concern about sex. Carlos had once told me sex is a natural beautiful act, something that must be done every day to stay healthy, kind of like brushing your teeth. Sophie gave us directions to Dick's house.

I was both fascinated, and sometimes repelled by the casualness of the local sexual attitudes. But who am I to judge? It had been that way for centuries and it accounted for the curious mélange of racial and ethnic cultures. It wasn't unusual for a couple who had been in bed together all night, to walk past each other in the light of day, and acknowledge one another with only the subtle rise of an eyebrow.

We found Big Dick sitting on his front porch with a magnificent view of the Philippine Sea, whittling on what appeared to be a piece of mangrove wood. There were dozens of handsome wood carvings of fish and maidens on the wall shelves. We introduced ourselves and shook hands. He wasn't surprised about our visit, and his English was above average. His Filipina love-mate brought us ice tea with calamansi, a plate of pineapples and tangerines and some homemade empanadas. He didn't introduce her but she nodded a greeting at us.

Carlos explained the purpose of our visit. Big Dick replied that he had been warned about us three hours before we showed up. Carlos asked how we should address him. Everyone including the men seemed to call him "Big Dick."

He said, "You can just call me Dick. That comes from Ricardo. The women started the Big Dick nickname about thirty years ago after my first wife died. I think she told the other ladies in their gossip sessions that I had a big *chili*. Since that time, I've been very lucky because many of the ladies wanted to find out if it was true. You just can't believe how horny some widows get."

I inquired, "You mind if I ask if the gossip is true? Seems like the whole matter is out in the open, and not a secret."

He answered, "I did okay as a young man. I'm an old man now, but I still take good care of my Filipina. As far as I know, she doesn't stray, and I don't either. She makes me happy."

Carlos asked, "Do the other women still hit on you?"

"Yep, that still happens. I just show it to them and get a quick blowjob. My Filipina doesn't get jealous if I don't fuck them."

I said, "You are definitely a legend on this island. Now, can we talk about the dog business? It's gotta stop."

"I knew this was going to happen, what with all the new rules and laws. Those politicos make it tougher every day to make a living. If I give it up, where will I get support for my family? And the damn stray dogs will be biting our kids, dumping over all the garbage cans, and snarling at passerby in the village."

I continued, "Just call Animal Control and maybe they'll trap some of the dogs and cats, and do an euthanasia. If nothing else, take all the dogs and cats down to the animal organization that does the sterilization for the critters. Then you won't get overrun with too many puppies and kittens."

"It's like supply and demand with drugs and whores. If the demand is there, it's going to be supplied somehow."

"The Korean tells me that he'll put a stop to it at his restaurant and maybe convince the others to do it also. There's plenty of crabs, lobsters, tuna and marlin in the wide Pacific for their menus."

He smiled, "Koreans love to eat dog. Good luck with that idea. If the Koreans stop, a lot of other Asians will keep eating the dogs, and maybe the supply will come from the Ponapeians and Chuukese. Some of them raise the dogs just for that reason."

Carlos asserted, "Dick, you have to stop or you'll end up arrested, and then your family will have tough times. How about selling your wood carvings at the airport? I know the tourists will snap them up. Good quality at reasonable prices. Your Filipina could sell them as the tourist planes come and go, or at the public markets."

"I'll try it. I can't imagine sitting in the jailhouse without my woman. I'd miss her and my new babies." Looking at his wife, he added, "Ain't she's a beauty and a good wife. And the best part, she keeps me feeling like I'm still in my twenties."

I laughed and said, "A good woman can do that. I know that experience."

Carlos concluded, "Oh yeah. I can relate. I have my own hot, witchy woman."

"Okay, you convinced me. I'll give the carvings a try."

As we were leaving, I said, "Dick, you better let those village ladies have a rest."

He winked and said, "An occasional blow-job is good for the soul… even the docs agree. A man has to have at least three orgasms a week to guarantee longevity." He paused and grinned, "Plus, I love it when they say 'I just wanna find out if the rumor is true.' It's my mission to satisfy their curiosity."

Once we were rolling back to town, I asked Carlos, "Do you think he'll give up the dog business? Perhaps we should buy some carvings to get his new business started."

He chuckled, "Depends on the tourists and his carvings, or if the Koreans offer extra money for more pups."

"Life goes on. Bow-wow!"

# 9

# SAIPAN HASH HOUSE HARRIERS (H-3)

At the hotel desk, we received a letter from the Grandmaster, Enrique "Coyote" Matagar, of the H-3 group in the Philippines asking if we could host an upcoming Hash Run which would involve most of the running clubs from the Far East Section. The run would include almost a thousand men (harriers) and women (hariettes or hussies) from the P.I., Malyasia, Japan, China, Thailand, Singapore, Indonesia, Nepal and India. The group had never been hosted in Saipan before. Tourism was down, so it would be easy to find other accommodations besides our Beach Hotel.

Cocina asked, "Tommy, what's the H-3, and why does their stationery say 'A Drinking Club with a Running Problem?' Are they a bunch of drunks?"

"You're going to love these folks. It's just a mixed-bag of people that get together informally to run off their eating and drinking excesses, and go from one point to the next through downtown areas, jungles, mountains, beaches and definitely bars for a cold beer or sparkling cold water. Some of them join for the exercise and social life and some join for one of the club objectives simply listed as 'to get laid.' There's always a lot of fun and adventures on their outings, some long-term matchups."

"Think they'll tear up our hotels if they get too borracho?"

"No worries. They're mostly responsible runners and athletes. It all started in Kuala Lumpur, Malaysia, 1938 when a group of Brits and other ex-patriates got bored and needed to get some exercise. They organized a run every week and named their exercise after the restaurant "The Hash House" inside the Salangor Club where many of the bachelors lived. The runners became known as the Hash House Harriers (H-3), and they developed a "pub crawl" as part of their program, always trying to find better food and colder beer than the monotony of the club's restaurant."

I continued, "When Japan invaded the Asian countries in World War II, H-3 lost its momentum, and didn't really emerge as a vigorous and mainstream club again until 1962 when Italy and Singapore started running clubs, and then it spread quickly to Australia and New Zealand. It has since become an international phenomenon with thousands of clubs with newsletters, directories and regional runs."

"How's it work. Do you have to an Olympic athlete to join? Can we give it a try, even us older people?"

"The clubs are open to everyone regardless of the physical fitness level and the members encourage others to get stronger and better; and they persuade older members that they're not as old as they feel. I've been in eight hashes, never came close to winning, but had more laughs and did more sweating than the gym anytime. Usually two runners called "hares" go out ahead of the group, known as "hounds" and lay out trails with plenty of dead ends and false leads. The front runner has to watch for clues along the way, like markers with paper or toilet paper signs, colorful ribbons, markers with chalk, flour or sawdust, or markings on the trail made with sticks or rocks."

Cocina said, "Sounds okay to me. I'll call around and see what the other hotel managers think." She paused, "Maybe you can talk to the Saipan hash contingent and see if they'll help out."

We met for lunch. Carlos and Daisy joined us with three bags of fresh mangos. Guangman took the bags off their hands and said that they would be ready for our dessert. Cocina said, "No problem with the other hotels. They have plenty of rooms and halls for the conference, but they want two days paid in advance on the reservations. Also they want a guarantee from the different clubs that all damage will be covered. That's standard for a big operation like this one."

"I talked to Juan Del Nero about the local hash kennel (chapter). He said his fifty plus members would help out anyway that they could." I continued, "And he invited us to the next run on Sunday. Juan and I have no idea where the run will take us but we meet at the downtown bank building. He said that the hares are young, athletic guys so it will probably be a tough event over the mountains onto some beach. Apparently the hares have a pattern of liking plenty of beer and barbeque close to the water at the end."

Carlos declared, "I'm game I've always wanted to try one of these crazy things. I've heard that they do some pretty stupid things at the end."

I laughed and said, "Hashers always like to say 'no rules' but there are some expectations that must be followed. If you stay with tradition, you probably won't be subjected to "punishment" at the end, like chug-a-lugging beer from a bed pan while they're chanting 'down-down.' If you stop drinking, they pour the rest over your head."

Cocina grimaced and said, "Tommy, that sounds real mature. How do you avoid the punishment?"

"Keep in mind, sometimes it's tough to avoid punishment if you're a newbie who's called a 'virgin' or a 'puppy.' You can't use real names, so until the hashers give you a hash name, you're referred to as 'Virgin', in your case as 'Virgin Cocina.' First timer Carlos would be called 'Virgin Carlos,' and so on. I picked up my hash name as "Tiger" on my fifth run, actually on the island of Pohnpei, because I growled at everyone after I downed my beer at one of the initiation rites. The informal rules say that you can't wear new shoes, no finger pointing of the real trail to others, and usually no children called 'horrors.' When you get on the run, you have to adopt a kind of a wild, carefree attitude, like 'I don't give fuck about anything.' Anything goes."

Carlos said, "I imagine a good number of people never come back for the second experience."

"Yep, that's true. It's definitely a few hours out of the week where we go a little wacko. But don't give up on the first hash, at least try it a second time. You might get into it and the zaniness."

Daisy asked, "What's the theme of the run on Sunday?"

I answered, "Besides being a tough one, everyone is expected to wear lingerie, and the trial will take us through downtown Garapan, the tourist district."

Daisy said, "I couldn't do that. It's too embarrassing in front of all those people."

"Just wear some none-see-through spandex gym shorts and a runner's bra underneath and your panties, silky bra, nighty, or whatever on top. It's all in fun. And remember in this whole thing, you won't have to do anything that you don't want to do, or you can cut out any time during the activities. It's easy to call a gypsy cab. It's meant to be fun and good-natured."

The week went by quickly and the anxiety level for Daisy and Cocina grew higher day by day. They got over the lingerie part but were worried that they couldn't keep up physically with the hash pack. I told them that Carlos and I would be with them the whole time, and sometimes it was better to be in the back of the pack so you didn't waste time and energy going down false trails.

When the momentous day arrived, it was a good turn-out of about seventy-five people wearing all colors and arrays of undies and tops. Some of the hussies even wore men's boxers and jock straps. The TV cameras were clicking away and the newspaper reporters were taking notes. Three of the newspaper ladies decided to join in and write their stories from inside the pack, rather than just being an observer and not knowing where the run might end. Carlos quipped, "Hell, they just want some cold beer." He was attired in a purple nighty.

I asked, "Where in the blazes did you find your size. I think you're larger than any woman on the islands."

"Had it custom made at Kaylene's tailoring shop. Where did you get your blue sexy nightgown?"

"Out of the hotel lost-and-found. I think one of our larger American lady guests left it in her room. It's kinda worn out, had a lot of use. Some unusual stains but I washed it good with bleach."

I looked over at Daisy and Cocina. Their little lingerie outfits of course, were beautiful, color-coordinated and fit perfectly. Damn, they were sexy women. They had found several mutual friends and were huddled up with a growing number of female runners.

The two hares took off to set the trail. The Saipan Grandmaster (known as "Coyote") called everyone to order and made sure that everyone had paid their fee and signed the liability waiver. He said that it would be rough trail and at the end of about five miles, the beer was guaranteed to be ice cold and plenty of it. Ten minutes later we were on the trail. The four of us stayed near the end of the pack. Both Daisy and Cocina had been working out and were easing along effortlessly. The foreign tourists along the roadways were laughing and waving.

I yelled over to Carlos, "I think they love my nightgown."

About a third of the way finished, the front pack of runners came up to us from the right after following a false trail. We followed in between them and ended up going over the highest mountain on Saipan, Mount Tapochau. Two-thirds finished, we were all sweating and singing the old children's story about the train that had to go up a steep hill "I know I can...I know I can..."

Topping out with a magnificent view of the multi-hued beaches, we started down a long slope to the ocean and spotted a fire and a dozen vehicles, mostly four-wheel drives. The smell of a barbeque and the thought of cold beer and water drove us in for a fast finish. I cautioned our little group not to volunteer their status unless they were willing go through with the initiation for newbies. The hash group started singing rowdy and bawdy songs that could be found in the Hash House Hymnal. The fellow leading the singing was known as the Religious Advisor (known as "Key", as in Key to Heaven) and he did ask if there were any new runners.

Carlos, being Carlos, raised his hand. I never stop admiring the outgoingness and fearlessness of the man. The group pulled him to the front of the circle in front of a large bonfire. The Religious Advisor told him that "to be a righteous hasher." the runner must prove himself worthy by downing a gallon of beer without taking a breath. Carlos looked over at us and said, "This is what I've waiting for!"

He almost chug-a-lugged it all except for a pint or two, and the Religious Advisor poured it over his head. Carlos yelled out, "Now cool on the inside and cooler on the outside." Most everyone unhitched their lingerie and tossed all the silkies into the fire, except for two mature ladies who had actually run in only panties and bras. America continues to be a wonderful country. Their bodies were firm and shaped like women in their early thirties.

The Religious Advisor said, "Time for chow and BBQ. Let's go!" The backup crew had been working all afternoon and the salads, tropical fruits and ribs were delicious beyond description, and extra tasty at beachside.

Some of the hashers continued on to their favorite bars as part of the evening pub crawl. We took a pass and hitched a ride in the back of a pick-up to get back to our car. I had made time to coordinate most of the upcoming events with the Grandmaster and Religious Advisor regarding our international hash hosting.

Carlos, I, and our wives managed to fit in another Hash Run before the conference. In one of her typical newly learned vernacular, Cocina said, "We've got 'to get our rear in gear' and be ready for the big conference run." The warm-up run was a round-the-island aqua endurance contest at high tide, which gave us a lot of water time, sometimes up to our necks in the lagoons. It was a lot of water-gurgling for our vertically-challenged Filipinas. The subsequent weeks went by quickly but Cocina and Front Desk Supervisor Myla found rooms for all the international entrants in various hotels, sometimes four to a room, plus conference halls for training and business meetings.

The island hotels were busy like before the 9-11 tragedy, and the restaurants and gift shops were so full that reserve staff had to be recruited. It was good for the economy. The police put on extra officers but nothing of significance developed, except for a few bar fights. The shady night-time ladies were busy and adding moolah to their bank accounts to send home to their families in the Philippines or China.

The night before the start, the thirty Grand Masters of the various running clubs met at the Beach Hotel for a briefing about the trail by the Saipan Team. Guangman prepared his special Korean coffee and Darjeeling tea, with huge platters of fresh-baked cinnamon rolls with the flavoring direct from the Micronesian cinnamon tree bark (Canela Molida). Cocina watched me eat three cinnamon rolls, rolled her eyes and patted her tummy, obviously referring to my waistline. I wrote off all the extra munching as necessary carbo-loading for the hash run. Besides, I watched Carlos eat the same amount, and neither of us wanted to insult Guangman's baking.

The big day arrived, and the meeting point was changed from the bank building to the American Memorial Park so there would be plenty of parking and the ever-needed porta-potties. The event took on a festive affair with quickly improvised barbeque and drink stands, and lots of island-made souvenirs for the visitors. T-shirt vendors were selling island shirts and shorts by the dozens. There were registrants from most of the Asian countries, and tourist runners who happened to be visiting from faraway lands such as Iceland, Kosova, Russia, Germany and France.

The Saipan hares took off to set the trail. Fifteen minutes later, a bugle blew and off went the eleven hundred runners. Many of us knew that eventually the run would do a giant circle of about eight miles and end up back at the starting point. Carlos and I jumped in the melee of runners, while Daisy and Cocina stayed back getting the food and drinks organized. They had even arranged for a local band to provide music on the concrete park stage. The back-up crews were barbequing burgers and hot dogs, and there were tubs and tubs of beer icing, along with water and juices. The weather was mostly clear with only an occasional light shower for cooling off the entrants.

The run immediately went to the top of the mountains, then followed a ridge trail requiring jumping over gulleys and creeks and then getting safely across several island thoroughfares. The fast runners managed to sidestep into several false trails but eventually got back to the main group. The course went all the way to the north end of the island, Marpi, and then came back along the waterline, before switching back to another mountain trail before dropping down to the ocean again and moving back into the park. Every time the runners crossed main drags, they were cheered on by hundreds of spectators. The paramedics were kept busy with cuts and bruises, and two of the runners had to be taken to the ER with broken legs.

Over nine hundred smiling, happy runners finished the course, including Carlos and myself. The Saipan Grandmaster took over the festivities on the park stage, congratulated everyone. We all received finisher medals with a hound dog prominently displayed in bronze. The Grandmaster then led the group in five songs about hashing and had volunteers relate some of their experiences. One of the American runners had found an empty grenade from World War II that had washed down from a mountaintop; a German runner proudly displayed a "boonie" dog that followed him on the entire course; and six Chinese runners did an improvised tai chi demonstration and dance, showing that they were still full of energy. Six "red-hatted" ladies did a darn good imitation of a French can-can dance. Each organization had to send up a newbie/virgin/puppy for the Saipan initiation and for punishment. It was a sight to remember to see about thirty male and female runners chug-a-lugging beer from chrome bedpans.

Two days later most of the hashers were gone, heading for new adventures on other islands or getting home to their job and family obligations. A cadre of the lads chartered a boat and went fishing up on the northern islands, mainly around Maug and Uracus; another bunch did a diving tour of Tinian and Rota; and as always, meeting one of the tenets of the organization, a dozen running couples decided they were in love and destined to be soul-mates, and about twenty of the runners fell in lust and love with the local gorgeous Chinese and Filipina women.

I asked Cocina, "Shall we host another big event?"

"Sure thing. My head is clear and my buns are tight. The next conference is in a quiet little tourist town called Pataya, Thailand. Should be fun. Talk Carlos into it. Daisy is excited about seeing new places."

Still no word where the missing governor might be.

# 10

## GIRLS, GIRLS, GIRLS

Former Public Safety Commissioner Lois Harding had left the island and returned to the mainland with her lawyer husband. She got home in time to enjoy a few hurricanes in the bayou along the Texas coast. The new commissioner, Joaquin Cruz, was a governor's crony but at least, he was trying to make things better on the island. One of my island buddies commented, "His heart is in the right place, now if he only has the brains to go with it." But after talking to him several times, I concluded that he was trainable and could make some improvements, like having the cops come to work for their assignments and not spending too much time with their girlfriends during the shifts when they showed.

Tourists were still being ripped off with car clouts and purse snatches, and the weak economy, and boredom, were driving too many of the young people into crime, particularly thefts and with fuel being so expensive, into siphoning gas. The slow economy was also impacting the ladies of the night, in that they were committing more bullshit thievery than usual with their customers, some even cutting their prices, selling marijuana, and several even tried blackmailing their "johns' by threatening to call the wives or the newspapers.

Since we had been married for over a year to our wives Cocina and Daisy, Carlos and I hadn't been in the bar scene recently and were not known by the new ladies. More likely, we would be recognized at the island concerts, stage plays, and even the ballet, with the artsy-fartsy crowd.  Our wives were doing their best to expose us to culture and the finer things in life.  By this time, we had probably lost our edge in bar billiards, table shuffle board, and beer guzzling.

And that's exactly what the Commissioner figured.  He called and asked if we could do some "decoying" in the bars as "a community service."  He had already obtained audio warrants so we could be wired up and the conversations recorded in a nearby police vehicle.  For a conviction, all the law requires is a proposition of sex of any kind for a fee.  If the mama-san does the arranging with the girl, either inside or outside of the bar, then she can be busted for procuring/pimping.  The ladies usually tried to slide out of their convictions by saying that they didn't understand English, yet they could convince the bar patron to buy a drink at an exorbitant price, negotiate  a sex deal with various positions and styles, and then arrange a ride back to their regular jobs the next morning.  With an audio warrant, all of this could be recorded, offsetting the language barrier argument    .

The foreign ladies are deported from the islands on the first violation of prostitution on the moral turpitude requirement.  They know about this, and going home in disgrace is not pleasant.  Thus, they'll just about do anything to get away, like running, biting and scratching, and offering free sex to the arresting officer just to let them leave the bar.  Most of the ladies are in their twenties and are agile and fast, and investigators are generally older and slower, which of course led to some interesting circumstances.

Carlos and I thought it was great fun to sit and yak with the ladies using government expense monies.  We hadn't figured on loud music and very bad karaoke singers.  We sat though hours and hours of off-key, self-proclaimed, non-Vegas-bound singers, including the working ladies who could hit a shrill note that vibrated through every corner of my brain.  On our first night, we got four clear-cut offers for sex in the same bar, with the mama-san making the final deal.  We signaled the waiting officers outside and in they came like gangbusters to make the arrests. Our instructions were to point out the ladies and then step back while the officers did the handcuffing.

One of the ladies had just finished with a previous customer and was coming out of the shower in the back hallway.  We hadn't received an offer of sex from her and had no intention of having her arrested. Carlos and I watched from the sidelines, as she quietly tip-toed out of the shower, completely naked carrying her panties, skirt and blouse. She made a bare-footed and bare-assed mad dash for a small ventilation window. She grabbed a chair for height, threw out her clothes and slid through the window, not hardly large enough for even a petite human being.

Carlos laughed, "Nice view. Very callipygian – nice shapely butt."

"Definitely a different version of a view window. Just another of life's many adventures. Stories to tell our grandchildren…after they become adults"

Carlos commented, "Very pretty girl."

"And clean too."

We heard her drop from the bar's second story, and saw her running through the backyards of the nearby residences, the overhead bar lights reflecting off her little white bottom. After she faded into darkness, we could still track her from the noise of the barking dogs as she ran through the residential yards. I said, "Hope those boonie dogs don't bite that beautiful butt."

Next night was a repeat of the first night, except it was a higher class joint and the ladies wore evening gowns. There were about ten ladies all dressed beautifully with perfect coiffures. Once we took seats in the bar, three ladies slid in next to us, enticing us to buy them expensive bar drinks, which was probably fruit juice or ice tea. They were liberal in showing off their female assets, letting their long dresses hike up, teasingly spreading their legs and saying in English, "We bad girls. We no wear our panties." Carlos said that he was in the mood for two or three girls, and soon we had offers from five of the ladies. When we gave the signal and the backup cops came running in, ten ladies, a manager and two bartenders ran in every conceivable direction. Carlos and I moved outside away from the commotion, and then spotted one of the ladies, slipping out from the tall bushes, and attempting to get over a ten-foot chain link fence in back of the club, wearing a long red evening dress and wearing high heels. She threw up her right leg on the chain-link and managed to get to the top and then spotted us. At first she was alarmed, then smiled and waved, and jumped off the fence and ran into the jungle.

Carlos yelled out, "That's a ten! What a great jump!" He smiled and added, "Nice dress but her mother would be upset about her going out without her panties."

I said, "That is one strong, determined woman. She's not even one of ours who made an offer."

Carlos smiled and said, "Let her run…let her run free! She deserves to get away."

"Amen, brother. If they had fence climbing in the Olympics, she'd be the winner."

Cocina is not a jealous type. But on the third night, she said, "I think maybe, just maybe, you boys are starting to have too much fun."

I smiled and answered, "All in the line of duty. Even President Obama said that volunteering is noble and makes the country run smoother. I'm just doing what's deep in my heart."

She chuckled and said, "Just keep everything inside those shorts." She gave my zipper a playful squeeze.

Apparently the "word" and our ID were not yet out on the street with our photos pasted up on the bar walls. Next night, Carlos and I walked into a poker arcade that allegedly offered more than video games and poker machines. It was like being thrown into a domestic fishing pond where the fish hadn't been fed for days. The ladies were all over us, offering to go to our rooms, do it in our rental car, or go in the back room for a blow-job. We picked out four that we liked and made our deal. When we signaled the outside cops to come and make the arrests, one of the ladies turned on me and said something in Chinese that likely translated to, "You fucking asshole. You're a gawd-damn cop." She tried to scratch my face and when I held her arms, she began biting me on the wrists. Carlos moved in to help me and we all fell to the tile floor. She was wiry and strong, and managed to move around and while trying for a very sensitive area to gnash, bit Carlos on both of his legs. The thigh bites were very close to the family jewels.

The DPS cops moved in and restrained her without any further problems. As she walked past me in handcuffs, she spit a major lugey on my shirt. Court records showed that she had already been ordered deported and was out on bail. This latest arrest would eliminate any of her chances for an appeal or mercy from the court. Being an all-around businesswoman, she was also carrying marijuana for sale.

Since the commissioner was becoming concerned about us being recognized in the Saipan bars, he asked us to go to the neighboring island of Tinian. Besides having fantastic beaches and diving spots, Tinian is best known as the island where Captain Paul Tibbits (1915-2007) and crew loaded up the atomic bomb in 1945 on the Stratofortress B-29 Enola Gay and dropped it on Hiroshima, basically ending World War II a few days later. The military has occasionally used Tinian for training and has plans of moving thousands of Marines to Guam, with the overflow going to Tinian.

There are fewer bars on Tinian and most of the customers are well known to the working ladies. When a stranger comes to town, it's likely the person is a tourist, possibly a government worker or special assignment or a cop. Thus, it often takes a few days for the girl to become acquainted before she'll make an offer of sex. In Carlos' case, he is well-known everywhere as a retired investigator, so there's a double whammy in that the regular local customers will tip off the girls that it might be a sting operation.

But Carlos got around that problem by acting drunk and stupid, and lighting up a joint that consisted of a special Asian tobacco that smelled like the real "Maui-wowi". He grabbed his crotch several times and yelled out, "I'm one horny bastard!" When the locals saw this, and that he was with a rich American partner, they just figured he was through with the law business and had just decided to become a "regular guy." The economy was flat and the ladies were broke and competitive for customers. They made their propositions within minutes. The lady with Carlos was topnotch on any scale and was wearing a stylish white blouse and skirt. We gave our signal and as the cops came in from outside, and the ladies and the bartender bolted for the doors and windows.

Carlos felt someone bump his rear pocket, and when he reached for his wallet, it was gone. The lady in white was floating over a pile of bodies, as swift and agile as any quarterback jumping over a line of guards and tackles, through the door and outside into the night. She was carrying something in her right hand, maybe a cell phone or more likely, Carlos' wallet. Carlos took off after her but he was slowed down by going through the pile of bodies rather than over the top. I followed close behind.

It had begun to rain heavily. The lady in white took off her high heels and ran like the wind. She was easily outrunning Carlos, but she made a classic blunder of looking back to see if Carlos was gaining. Her left foot hit the sharp edge of the asphalt roadway and off she went vaulting into a huge puddle of mud and rain water in a giant belly flop. She landed facedown, knocking the air out of her lungs. Carlos pulled her to her feet to stop her from drowning, and walked her back to the police. I found his wallet along the road, close to where she had thrown her shoes.

I spotted a beach towel behind the bar top and gave it to her to wipe off some of the mud so we could see her face for the mug shot. Her long black hair was falling in thick stringlets, covered with dripping mud. Fortunately she had only a few minor bruises and scrapes on her face. Carlos telephones her friend to bring some clean clothes to the police station. The matron got her showered up and then we chatted in the briefing room. She was trying to have a sense of humor and said, in broken Chinese, "I know I can outrun you guys. You're very big and slow."

Carlos winked at me and said, pretending gruffness, "Yeah, maybe, but can you outrun my police radio or one of my bullets?"

Chinese subjects are often frightened by the police. They're not sure what "the official police" can do or will do when they are handcuffed. Some of them are so scared when they go to jail, which they call the "monkey house," that they wet their pants or go catatonic, than are surprised when they actually go to court in 24 hours to hear the charges and have a chance to bail out and have a lawyer and a translator. There are no rapes or beatings from the guards. It is a very confusing process for the ladies being from a communist country.

Carlos' comment made the lady very contrite. She apologized profusely and lowered her eyes to the floor.

Carlos smiled and walked her back to the matron. He said, "Don't worry. You'll be fine…just don't be stealing any more wallets. The next man may get really angry and smash you to the floor."

As she left with the matron, "I know. I'm sorry. I won't do it again."

I asked, "Do you think that's true?"

"Maybe. She's into survival for her and her family. I saw the money transmittal forms in her purse. She's been sending money home regularly to her family in Shanghai."

"On to the next case, Sherlock."

Carlos asked, "Do you think Holmes and Dr. Watson ever worked prostitution cases?"

"Probably not. They just visited the brothels... and they liked the opium dens too, and a little tad of cocaine, Old Boy."

Carlos chuckled and said, "Tom, you've been reading those British biographies again."

"Nope, not this time. It's the Discovery channel, my young laddy."

Our next assignment was back on Saipan in a drive-by operation in our beat-up, rusty Camry, checking out chicks in mini-skirts and high black boots. Apparently the street ladies were flagging down cars and trucks at a major intersection. The male drivers enjoyed the occasional flash of a breast or bottom. Some of the tinted vehicles carried families, which was upsetting to the wives, especially when the street ladies looked inside and called the driver by his first name.

Carlos and I drove by several times to get an idea how many ladies were working. We spotted about ten, some back in the shadows. Several of the ladies had been in the bars when we made the previous arrests. We both knew if we drove up like potential customers, we would "be burned" before we said hello.

Carlos asked, "Wanna have some fun?"

"Call it. Always ready for a little joy and happiness."

"Here we go. Roll down the window so they see us and get ready to exit real fast."

Carlos drove at double-speed right to the ladies on the corner. He shouted to me, "Here we go!"

As the car stopped about ten feet in front of the group, the first three ladies spotted us, gasped and screamed in Chinese to alert the others, and ran like hell. There were more women in the shadows than we had suspected, and soon there about fifteen desperate, determined ladies running, mostly in clappity-clop high heels, for any kind of concealment. No one wanted to be arrested. Of course, they had been soliciting the male tourists for sex but on this evening we had no sustainable probable cause for arrest.

One of the younger gals ran into a dead-end small alley and tried to hide behind a small bush in a planter. She had her eyes closed, probably figuring if she couldn't see me, then I couldn't see her. I walked over to her and when I tapped her on the shoulder, she let out a yelp and almost fainted. She wet her pants. When I gestured that she could leave and again, I thought we had found another contender for the London Olympics. She was gone in a flash.

Back at the car, Carlos said, "I think we cleared up the street walker problem for the night. They're gone until tomorrow."

"Kind of reminded me of quail hunting. When the dog kicks up a covey, the birds go flying in every direction. I never which one to aim for and end up missing every bird."

Carlos got a call on his cell phone. It was the commissioner and he asked if we could stop by the Top Dog Bar in San Antonio. He had an interesting case for us to double-check.

Arriving at the bar, we saw that half the cops were laughing while the other half was hard with work working a possible homicide scene with photos and measurements. The commissioner informed us that a former high-level politician had died during a blow-job in back of the bar. The neighbors heard a girl screaming in Chinese and called 911. When the patrol officers arrived they found the hysterical woman out front saying that there was a dead guy in back. When the officers got everything sorted out, it appeared that the dead guy was an elderly regular and came in every Tuesday night when his wife went off to play bingo. The commissioner showed us the body and the male adult victim was clearly looking up into the sky with a wide, contented smile.

The commissioner explained what his cops were doing and they had everything covered. They transported the nineteen-year-old "blower" girl down to the police station and took a formal statement accompanied by a Chinese translator. She said that the victim had told her that he was seventy years old with a heart condition, and wanted her to give him a soft, gentle blow-job. The girl said that just as he climaxed in her mouth, he made a loud sigh and said, "Thank you." Then he tumbled over and died.

The commissioner, Carlos and I chatted in the hallway. The commissioner said that there were no signs of injury on the victim, and that he had checked with the man's local doctor. He did have a heart condition and needed a triple-bypass which he kept delaying. The commissioner said, "I can't see any charges against the girl. I'm going to let her go."

I said, "You sure can't charge her with prostitution. There's no witness to testify in court and he won't be complaining."

Carlos chuckled, "Yeah, there's a charge…a felony in fact. How about assault with a dangerous mouth?"

I added, "And just think if she can kill with that young mouth now, how dangerous will she be when she's an experienced, mature woman."

The new officer that had been assigned to make the death notification arrived. He said to the commissioner, "Well, I did it. My first one. It wasn't so bad." The newbies generally get the rotten job of making notifications to the decedent's family.

The commissioner said, "How did it go?"

"The wife just frowned and said, 'That silly old fool. I told him to stop going down to that bar.' She shook my hand and said she would go the hospital and make arrangements for the body."

I said, "Case closed."

The commissioner said, "Mahalo to you guys for your help. You are "toast" for now in the decoy business. Too many ladies know your ugly mugs. Maybe we can do this again in a year or two."

We waved goodbye. No more drinking on government money. I mentioned, "Damn, I was enjoying nookie patrol."

Carlos said, "Yeah kinda but maybe my karaoke headache will be gone by next year."

# 11

## ON THE ROAD AGAIN

Augie finally came up with an acceptable contract to find the missing governor and return whatever we could find of the embezzled 4.5 million dollars and get it back to the dwindling commonwealth treasury, less our twenty percent. The contract got rid of all the legal gobbledygook, was clean, neat and understandable, and clearly stated the expectations of both parties, the Agency and the Government. It could have been easily written by an articulate English 101 student and would have saved a lot of precious time, and legal fees.

Carlos and I bought our tickets on Continental Micronesian Airlines for the island hopper through Micronesia. Temporarily we skipped Palau and Yap, knowing that the missing governor didn't speak those languages and had no ties to any of the islands in their environs. The local people on those islands would notice him right away, being an outsider. He wouldn't blend in and there would be a lot of chatter on the coconut radio.

After Guam, our first stop was in Truk now known by the old traditional name of Chuuk. The State of Chuuk, in the country of the newly formed Federated States of Micronesia, consists of eleven major islands and forty-four small islets, and forms one of the largest lagoons in the world, about fifty by thirty miles, nearly 3130 square kilometers. It's about seven degrees about the equator and typically hot and humid.

During World War II on February 17, 1944, American forces sunk over sixty ships of the Japanese Imperial Fleet, destroyers, cruisers and freighters, which included the submarine 1-169 Shinohara, which had taken part in the attack on Pearl Harbor in 1941.

Since that time, the ships have developed their own eco-systems in and around the hulls and decks, and the old ships are homes to millions of fish and other sea life. The ships are also the respected tombs of thousands of Japanese sailors who went to the bottom of the lagoon after the attack.

New laws now protect the contents of the ships and the remaining human skeletons, and this world-famous wreck diving destination has the policy of "Look but Don't Touch." It's not unusual to see fish and other sea creatures swimming and crawling around rusty bulldozers, trucks, torpedoes, and huge guns that will stay on the ships for eternity. Laws have also been legislated that stops all fishing with explosives. In the past, the local fisherman had taken explosives from the ships, and then set them off on the reef. This type of "fishing" sent thousands of dead fish and crustaceans to the surface and destroyed significant parts of the reef. Several fishermen also killed themselves in the explosions, not knowing how to safely handle the ordinance. One man on the island is called "Lefty" as he mopes about with a missing left hand and wrist and doing handyman jobs along the waterfront.

Oceanographer Jacques Cousteau explored the Chuuk Lagoon in 1969, and made a subsequent movie which put this part of Micronesia on the map for all diving enthusiasts. His documentary called "The Ghost Fleet of Truk" made Chuuk world-famous and showed how effective the newly designed "aqua lung" was for deep-water diving.

Carlos and I did a quick shallow dive in the morning and a snorkeling outing in the afternoon. We managed to check out five ships underwater. We had a dual purpose with the diving, the first of course was to explore the pristine lagoon and soak up the splendor, and the second was to meet a lot of the locals and pick up any gossip that might be circulating about the missing governor from Saipan. We talked to dozens of locals and never came across anyone that had even heard of Ignacio. Technical communication and newspapers are close to non-existent in Chuuk, and just about everyone was ignorant about the economic plight in Saipan. The people on Chuuk had their own problems with less US funding and tourist arrivals, and more corruption from the officials.

We stopped in the popular bars, and knowing that we couldn't fly until twenty-fours after diving, had a late night, and met a visiting mainlander nurse named Christy Thompson from Connecticut in the Last Resort Cocktail Lounge. The bar's drink on special was called "The Wet Cocksucker."

Blonde, busty Christy said, "Good name for a drink, eh? I've already had three, drinks I mean, not cocks." Christy was an inebriated, free spirit and looking for a bed partner for the night. We told her that she was beautiful with a great personality but we were both married and intended on keeping our marriages alive, and our bodies intact. Christy wasn't about to let it go. She slurred, "Looky here, who would know? There's no good guys for fucking on this gawd-damn rock."

Carlos just shook his head. I replied, "Christy, you might just have to wait until you get home on the mainland. You've got a boyfriend there, right? How could you not have a sex buddy?"

"Carlos, you're right on, but I'm used to having a little physical fun every day. You know us nurses. We know all the sensitive spots and like to use them."

"He'll be waiting for you. He'll be horny too, and you can have another honeymoon."

I said, "You've got fingers. That's probably what your lover-boy is doing until you get home. You can a lot of fun on the phone."

"I'm tired of that. I usually get in my rental car, drive around, crank up the music with rock-and-roll, and reach down in my shorts with my magic thumb. When I get to a private spot on the island, I just let it go and scream like blazes. It's okay, but now I want the real thing." She paused and added, "And you guys are nice and decent looking, and will be gone in a few days. No gossip. I'm still here for another lonely ten days. How about a tumble, both of you if you want!"

I said, "No can do."

Carlos affirmed, "Same here, but we enjoy talking to you."

"Thanks, Guys, but right now I need more."

She got up and left. We heard her car start up and saw her driving in the direction of the darkest, remote end of the island. I said, "Looks like she going to handle the 'need' in her own way."

"Tom, if I see her tomorrow, I'm going to ask her what her favorite songs are when she reaches her nirvana. I might buy some of that music for Daisy. She tells me she gets real lonely when I'm gone and takes a lot of cold showers."

"Cocina has her own deflection system – it's called teenagers. She says when I'm gone, it takes all her energy just keeping track of those characters. When the day is done, she just tumbles into bed for a nice, long sleep."

The next day, we talked to the church officials and visited some of the tourist sites. Many of the old Japanese artillery guns were still in place along with trenches and underground bunkers. The Japanese had planned on staying for a long time and had built impressive defensive bulwarks, using Micronesian slave labor. We found piles of old sake bottles, prompting Carlos to say, "So we now know how the Japanese lost the Big War. Looks like they were party animals and not paying attention to the American bombers."

One of Carlos' classmates from the police academy days, Jorge Castro, waved us down on the main drag. After introductions, Jorge asked if we wanted to go on a marijuana farm suppression mission on the nearby island of Tol. Carlos smiled at me, and I smiled back, nodding in the affirmative. Offering police action to a cop is even more tempting than one of Guangman's fresh donuts. I said we would follow Jorge to the harbor and meet up with the police boat.

After leaving in the police boat for the ninety minute ride to Tol, Jorge explained that one of the many contributions by the US Peace Corps was the introduction of Hawaiian marijuana seeds for fast-growing eight-foot plants with a high THC content, locally known as "Maui-Wowee" or 'Powee-Wowee" or by the Japanese name of "Maru." It was jokingly told that it was not an official part of the Federal Program, but it was certainly effective in developing a productive and appreciated crop for the local people. Old grandmothers often said, "I'd rather see the youngsters smoking weed, than drinking beer, and going crazy with alcohol." The grandmothers were known to light up also. As Jorge explained, I was soon to see "topless grannies" on Tol sitting around a campfire, smoking grass and singing ancient tribal songs.

The Chuuk cops had been told there were 800-900 mature marijuana plants ready for harvesting. Personal use of marijuana was not a problem but the large operations were smuggling the weed across international borders into Guam and Japan. The DEA had asked for help. As we approached the island, the growers bounced a few .22 caliber rounds off the front of the boat, not intending to kill or injure the cops, just scare them. The boat slowed slightly and did a zigzag to shore. The cops, including Carlos and myself, put on our bullet-resistant vests and sat on the floor below the bulwark, not wanting to catch a ricochet. As we docked, we saw several dozen marijuana plants going up and over the first hill. Obviously there was a person inside of each plant holding the trunk, but all we could see was "running" marijuana plants through the thick growth of jungle terrain.

The cops secured the plants that were still on the beach farm, and then went hunting for the forty to fifty plants, judging by the holes in the ground, that "ran away." The escaping plants were found on the other side of the hill, buried in some beach driftwood. One of the island residents said, "We need the crop. It means money for us to buy rice and chicken. We never expected you guys would chase after the plants." He chuckled and said, "Most of you hombres look too fat to climb a hill." Citizens often think fit cops are fat, mainly because they don't realize how bulky a protective vest can be.

No arrests were made, because surprisingly, no one knew anything about marijuana cultivation. One of the only three high-powered pickups on island drove up to the officers. The mayor exited the truck. We knew he was the mayor because the title was embroidered on his baseball cap. He had the most magnificent protruding potbelly over his belt and was wearing only flip-flops and a pair of faded blue shorts. He asserted that he was totally bewildered about marijuana growing on his island and promised to check into it. His "innocent" look could have won an Emmy.

The cops did some plant chopping with long, sharp machetes and loaded the plants into the police boat, and off we went back to the main island, Weno, where the police headquarters was located. Photos were taken for possible later court action, and the pile of freshly-cut weed was covered with BBQ light fluid for quick ignition. Before the torch was even lit, a large crowd of islanders swarmed the area. They all stood downwind, expecting a "free high" via the courtesy of the government.

Supply and demand always play a role in prices on the black market. Chuuk was no exception - the price of a marijuana cigarette doubled before the sun had set.

During the report writing session after the marijuana suppression operation, Carlos told Jorge about the "needy" hospital nurse Christy. He chuckled and said, "I know just the guy. He's my brother-in-law, Johnny-Boy, just back from the mainland. He spends half his day in the gym, and the rest of the day hunting for available felines. Sounds like she just wants a 'wham-bam, thank-you ma'am,' and Johnny could be the guy. He'll give Christy a memorable island experience."

I gave him Christy's blonde, busty description and the information about the Last Resort Bar. He called Johnny-Boy on the phone. After he hung up, he said, "Done deal. Johnny is on a mission. He's happy – she'll be happy. What could be better?"

Carlos summarized, "All in the line of duty. It's our job to make the citizenry happy."

"Amen, my Brother."

Later in the evening, Jorge invited us to his home for a delicious meal of sashimi and rice and cold, cold Sapporo Japanese beer. His wife, Marianna, was a beautiful woman and a wonderful hostess. She laughed out loud when Jorge told her about her brother, Johnny-Boy, going to find Christy. She commented, "I know Christy from the Chuuk hospital. She's going to be one tired girl."

Carlos explained that we were looking for the missing governor, Ignacio Antolin, and millions of embezzled dollars. Jorge had heard of the governor but he asserted that the chances of him being found anywhere in the Chuuk islands were unlikely. He said the boats going back and forth from the Western, Mortlocks, or Hall Islands would have carried the word to Weno. He laughed and added, "Next to sex, gossip is one of the more important activities of the day."

I asked, "Any ideas about what we should do to find the governor?"

Jorge answered, "I'm going to introduce you to one of the most colorful guys you will ever meet. His name is Captain Yancey Hilton and he skippers a dive boat called the Shark's Tooth. He knows most of the Micronesian islands, even the ones that just show at low tide.

If anyone can find the governor hiding on a remote island, he's the man."

Carlos said, "He might be a big help. How can we contact him, Jorge?"

"First, let me tell you a bit about Hilton before you decide on hiring the man. He is a mondo bizarro dude, a little weird for being the head honcho of a very expensive boat, but he knows how to navigate in and out of lagoons with very narrow openings in the coral reef and he's good with the tourists and the local islanders. He loves to sing and dance. However, be prepared for off-the-wall behavior. He enjoys his independence and he really likes his beer."

I said, "We'll meet him and decide. We need his help and he'll be more effective than fly-overs with surveillance planes."

"No problem. I invited him for dinner." He paused and pointed, "Here he comes now – late as usual."

I looked over to the front gate and saw a blonde, long-haired man, wearing sun-whitened khaki shorts and a muscleman gym shirt, coming our way. I said to Jorge, chuckling, "He's got the day and date right. He's just on island time, which means any time."

Walking behind him was a stereotype, gorgeous Southseas woman in a bright red sarong. She glided towards us in a pure natural form with her long hair swaying, walking as though she was a slight breeze gracefully blowing through the jungle. She was tall, light-skinned and had Caucasian features. She was braless and her wide feet were encased in the flimiest of sandals.

# 12

## SAILING WITH CAPTAIN HILTON

The old saying "not judging a book by its cover" truly rang true with Captain Hilton. If you came across him on street in an urban area, you'd automatically cross to the other side of the street, or duck into a store until he went past. He wasn't exactly ugly or evil looking, but seemed to have an aura about him that translated to trouble if you ever disagreed with him or tried to take advantage of him or his friends. He was macho and primitive, and he swaggered. He respectfully introduced his woman as Sally from the State of Pohnpei. She acknowledged us by subtly raising her eyebrows, island style.

Captain Hilton didn't have a legal wife or family, but without hesitation or embarrassment, he explained Sally was from Ngatik (native name of Sapwuahfik), an island in Pohnpei. She stayed with him on shore and was a dive instructor when the boat went to sea. They had been together for over ten years. Accounting for her features and skin tone, he explained that a British whaling ship went to Ngatik in 1837 and the crew killed all the males so that they could have all the women to themselves. He added, "Over the years, fair-skinned Britishers mated with the local brown females, and my Sally here, is one of the beautiful results."

She smiled and threw him a kiss. She and Jorge's wife went off into the shadows to enjoy a bottle of tuba, fermented coconut juice.

First impressions are often negative and unreliable, and we soon found that was the case with Captain Hilton, or Yancey as he liked to be called. For all his physical coarseness, he was well-read and up-to-date on the news. He ate his meal slowly, had a few beers, and settled back to talk about the missing governor. Backing up Jorge, he repeated that he'd bet a million dollars that Ignacio wouldn't be found anywhere in Chuuk State. He said that Weno was the home base and anchorage for his boat, the Shark Tooth, and that he had recently visited many of the outer islands on diving expeditions and half his crew members were from outlying islands, and they would have seen or heard everything about the remote areas.

Carlos asked him if he would be willing to help search for the missing governor, probably in neighboring Pohnpei, possibly on one of the outer islands like Pakin, Ant Atoll, Mokil (Mwoakilloa), Pingelap, or one of the Polynesian Islands within the state boundaries, Nukuoro or Kapingamarangi, all roughly part of the Caroline Islands chain.

Yancey said it could be done. "We already know Ngatik is not a probability because Sally would have heard. The other islands are hundreds of miles part and it would take a long time to get there. You might consider renting a seaplane, that could come down from Guam."

I said, "Tell us about your boat, and maybe if it's large enough, you could still take along guests for diving at some of those spots that divers seldom experience."

"The Shark Tooth is Ice Class Antarctic Whaler built in Norway in 1954, and was used for breaking through ice to hunt for whales. It's 170-foot long, 1100 tons, holds 100,000 gallons of fuel, and accommodates twenty-two guests in eleven rooms. The maximum speed is about seventeen knots. We have FAX machines, email, telphones, radio, DVD and VHS, and most of the comforts of home. We've got about 18,000 gallons of potable water. There's two dive 30-foot launches aboard that can get into small inlets and over shallow reefs. We have NITROX blends of air and most equipment you would need for diving or fishing." Throwing out his chest, he said, "You know one of the best part of a trip on the ship? It's my staff of twenty who cater to your every need, plus they know the best dive spots, can fix an engine, bind up a wound, and so on. They're just a good bunch of people, very kicked-back and guest-oriented, mainly islanders from throughout Micronesia, even a guy from Fiji, a dynamite mechanic."

Carlos stated, "Sounds fun, luxurious and seaworthy, but I heard you hit a reef near Pohnpei, and did extensive damage."

"That's true unfortunately, over a year ago, but she's shipshape now. We didn't damage the reef or cause any oil spills. We spent a lot of money and time fixing her up in a Philippines shipyard, and she's as good as new, maybe even stronger. We've already taken her out for a dozen week-long voyages with guests aboard. She performed magnificently."

I asked, "How about fuel? Those islands are spread out over wide expanses of the Pacific. Not too many fuel depots."

"Tom, we burn a combination of diesel fuel and the residue from the electrical plants from around the islands. The Shark Tooth is a steamship, and we create a miniscule of pollution, actually burning up the discarded afterburn materials from the power plants. So, every time we visit an island where there's a large generator, we end up with more fuel, and the locals are glad to find a way to get of their afterburn residue."

Carlos asked, "Whatsa think? Want to help us on our Pacific high seas adventure? Be something different."

He asked Sally to come join our group. He said that he was inclined to go on the manhunt, adding, "She's number one partner in my book. She's also my financier, bookkeeper and profit wizard." He explained everything to Sally and she nodded in the affirmative. Now it was a matter of setting the right price. The weather was good and the ship was ready to go. The price was finally negotiated out at twenty thousand dollars per week, with another thousand for food. Anyone in our group that wanted to go diving, time permitting, would pay extra and work out the fee with the diving instructor or guide. Jorge asked to go for no pay, using up his vacation time from his work. We felt a little more comfortable and safer with a legally, armed policeman aboard.

Yancey exclaimed, "Aye, Laddies. He'll keep the thieving pirates at bay!"

We toasted one another with the ladies' tuba. When it was gone, Yancey reached inside his pack and brought out a new bottle of "Jose." After the bottle went around several times, there were no longer any problems associated with snakebite, scurvy or tuberculosis. I added a few Filipino cigars to the festivities to help chase away the marauding mosquitoes.

Next morning, five of the ship's staff said they would go without pay, just to see all the new islands. Three paying guests from Germany came along at $2500 each per week. They were all retired businessmen with no schedules to keep.

The sense of adventure was catching. The next twenty-four hours was a mad scurry of getting everything aboard for a long voyage, particularly finding enough spare parts should something break down in the middle of the ocean. Sally kept a thorough check-off list. We promised everyone a bonus if we found the governor and got some money back for Saipan.

# 13

## ON TO POHNPEI, THE GARDEN ISLE

Next morning, we steamed our way over endless miles of open ocean, aptly giving Micronesia the nickname of the "Land of Sea," with very few little islands and fresh water ports. This part of the Pacific spawns more tropical typhoons that any other place on the earth, an average of nineteen per year, with many of them making their way to the Philippines and Japan. Our destination was Pohnpei (meaning "high place" in the local language – top of a volcano) about halfway between Honolulu and Manila.

Pohnpei, known as Ponape until 1984, is hot and humid and averages two hundred inches of rain along the coastline, and some four hundred inches of rain – no one knows for sure - at 2,540 feet on Nahnalaud (Big Mountain) and Ngihneni (Giant's Tooth). The high peaks catch the passing clouds and wring the water out of them, resulting in forty-two streams and long, wide rivers, and abundant, ever-flowing waterfalls. The crystal-clear pools of fresh water at the bases provide excellent swimming holes, and habitat for fish and eels.

Besides its natural splendor, Pohnpei is also an interesting footnote in the history of the Civil War. Weeks after the Confederate surrender at Appomattox, the Confederate armed raider Shenandoah sailed into the Pohnpei harbor and discovered four Yankee whalers. The raider's mission was to sink the Union whaling fleet in the Pacific to stop oil from getting to the North for lamps and lubrication. The raider sunk these ships and went on to burn and destroy another thirty-four Yankee ships and took over a thousand prisoners, sailing all the way to Alaska. Once it was discovered that the War was over, the Shenandoah dropped its guns and armament, and managed to escape to England.

Pohnpei is both mysterious and ominous with the mist-shrouded peaks and dark coastal mangrove forests, and yet when it stops raining and the sun comes dancing through the foliage, the island takes on a magical glow with its lush, tropical, broad-leaved plants, and giant ferns and betel nut palms. A saying in local lore translates to, "When Pohnpei's bright orange hibiscus flower falls prey to the tropical sunlight, it turns saffron yellow, tinged by burgundy, more elegant in death than in life…" Flowers are everywhere, and so are bright, happy children running through the jungle. The classic greeting in Pohnpei is *Kaselehlia,* which has a meaning of hello and welcome, like the Hawaiian greeting Aloha; and we soon learned the friendly people meant every syllable.

While making our way to Pohnpei, I used every communication device on the Shark's Tooth, and got hold of a dozen of my financial and business contacts in California. I soon found that Ignacio Antolin had stashed almost a million dollars in his daughter's name and had transposed her first and middle names, and used his wife's maiden name of "Barbosa" for the account. The money had been deposited from various locations in the US, Caribbean islands and Europe, always in small amounts under ten thousand dollars not causing the intrusion of the IRS into the account. I had a banking friend place an unofficial hold on the bulk of the account, and not wanting to attract attention from Ignacio, allowed the wife to make withdrawals up to five thousand dollars.

As we slipped through the break in the reef into the Pohnpei harbor, Yancey pointed out the spot about a hundred yards away, where the Shark's Tooth had crashed her bottom on the reef. He said that it had happened at low tide when he was too busy taking care of his guests, and not giving his complete attention to his route. Others said he was halfway through a blowjob from a fashion model when the ship struck the reef, and his little soldier was almost severed by the girl's teeth.

While showering topside, some said that they had seen the ugly, scary scar left by the girl's gnashers.

However, today was no problem, and we docked safely next to Takatik Island where the airport is located. As the crew was tying the ship to the wharf, the dock area was suddenly alive with vendors, pimps, guides, taxis, government officials, and a welcoming committee of gorgeous island women with mwars-mwars and leis.

Yancey laughed and said, "In the early days, the ladies would have come out to the ship in canoes, and traded their mahogany-tinted bodies for tobacco and any kind of metal. They would stay on the ships until sailing day, which was okay with the local men because it was a very relaxed society with sex and lust, and the best part was that the men could fashion axes and shovels from the metal. The sad consequences of all this free love, of course, was that the natives had no resistance to European diseases, and many of them died because of measles, TB and syphilis. A neighboring island called Kosrae lost ninety percent of their population to STD's, and a result, it became a very conservative, highly religious society fashioned after the New England protestant churches of previous centuries."

I commented, "At least we can still see their beauty and their femininity...and those hips."

Yancey smiled, "Yep, that's true. You can go crazy thinking about riding those hips. Now the women mostly work for the tourist agencies and many of them are going to the local college... but there's still plenty of island fun when the sun goes down."

Carlos said, "Definitely true on Saipan, and about the same in California when I was taking classes. Boys like girls everywhere, and vice-versa."

I asked, "What's our next step, Yancey?"

"We have to clear customs and immigration, which will be easy, because they all know me and the ship after so many trips. Then we go and talk to the federal cops in Palikir, and then the local guys in Kolonia Town. After we do that, it will be gossip and yak-yak at the local bars like "Cupid" and "Palm Terrace." We'll be the talk of the town, and everyone will know why we're on-island in about an hour."

We filled out a few simple forms and after the Pohnpei officials made a cursory check of the ship, we were waved ashore. We were booked at the Village Hotel, an eco-friendly, grass-shack-looking hotel a few miles out of town. While the island workers from the ship drifted off with their friends, the hotel van took us and the German guests to the hotel. For almost fifty years, the hotel had been owned and managed by a happy, enthusiastic couple from California, Jon and Danni Lafferty. They had a rental car lined up for us so we could go exploring and "talk up" the missing governor at the remote villages.

I asked, "Do you already know why we're here?"

Jon laughed, "Sure, everybody knows. You won't find Ignacio Antolin here on island. He was here about three weeks ago, and then just disappeared, probably to some remote tiny islet. I don't think he left Micronesia. He's not the type to stay in Europe or Australia. He's an island boy and just wants to live a simple life. He still has some distant family members here."

Carlos asked, 'Jon, what do you suggest?"

"Just stay low profile for a week or so, and let the coconut radio carry the gossip around the entire island and off into the outlying islands. I'd offer a thousand dollar reward. If he's here, we'll get the word. Meanwhile, enjoy the island. There's a fifty-mile paved road that goes all the way around the island…lots of scenic spots and waterfalls, and some good country "mom-and-pop" stores where you can get fresh fish and vegetables, and any kind of tropical fruit that you want. The local ladies serve up scrumptious meals. When we're traveling in Paris or London, I often get daydreaming about the good island food."

Danni joined us. The tropics had been kind to her. She was still lean and healthy, and had the skin and complexion of a much younger woman. She attributed her youthful appearance to daily applications of fresh coconut oil. Her form of basic English would rival that of any truck driver, anywhere. Until I talked to her, I never the knew the F-word could mean so many things, anything from making love to messing with somebody to masturbating. Listening to Danni talk about life and people, especially about politicians, was truly a "fuckathon." There was no other way to explain it. I watched Jon out of the corner of my eye, and I knew he was enjoying a new audience react to Danni.

She exclaimed, "Look, you Guys, the chance of finding Ignacio is like fucking zero. His fucked-up family won't turn him in, and he's probably out fucking some stupid bitch in the fucking jungle."

I know Carlos only too well with his unique sense of humor. I knew he had to ask, "Danni, we've got a fucking job to do. Any ideas how or where we can find this fuckhead?"

Guffawing, Danni was into it. "Carlos, I don't really care about the fucker or that fucked-up Saipan. But I'm willing to help you because I already like you guys. I know Jon recommended a reward…this fucking place is so poor that the locals would turn in their own fucking mother for cash. They're that fucked up."

"What else?"

"Do what you're doing right now, just fuck around for a few days. Some fuck-brained asshole will get the word to you about Ignacio. Just so you know, I never liked that fucker. He was always kind of sleazy."

We finished out the fucking evening with a boiled giant coconut crab at the fucking bar…really fucking delicious. I don't suppose the crab agreed.

# 14

## THE SCREAMING HAOLE WAHINE

During our stay on Pohnpei, life took on its own relaxed momentum as we made inquiries from village to village about the missing governor. Being far out in the jungle, we were treated to experiencing untouched nature at its finest, with gorgeous flowers and thick foliage of a zillion shades of green. Most of the villagers were into subsistence farming or fishing. Life was easy but boring if you have an active disposition. As with other island cultures, gossip remains right behind food and sex in importance to the villagers in these remote areas.

Around a campfire one night just below Mount Nahnalaud`, Carlos and I heard about a blonde, stereotype Scandinavian woman, Sammie, who came to work for the Pohnpei Legislature as a recorder. She was head-turner with long straight hair and bodacious legs that went "all the way to the top floor." Her boyfriend Roy also came along but he seemed dull and non-descript next to her, and basically went unnoticed. At least, he was anonymous for awhile. Roy did odd jobs whenever he could find work, while his girlfriend was the center of attention and very well-paid by the government.

Carlos and I had met them several times in the local Japanese restaurant. She was every bit the beauty and he, well, he was a just average-looking guy from the mainland.

Sammie and Roy rented an open Samoan-type house on the edge of the jungle near the main town of Kolonia.  It was a quiet area, and unless the wind was blowing or the rain falling, it was basically soundless.  Occasionally you might hear a coconut falling from a tree or a huge rat scurrying across the roof. As soon as they moved in, strange, eerie high frequency noises were reported in town that were described scary and resounding mysteriously through the jungle.  Being superstitious, the locals thought it might be ghosts searching for their past loved ones.  Several American men were not into mumbo-jumbo, and snuck through the jungle at night trying to decipher the strange high-pitch noises.

Once they heard it, the experienced Americans recognized the noise right away, and at the next gossip session mentioned that it was just two romantic people in love.  The local lads did a recognizance and soon discovered that Sammie and Roy were madly in love and lust and were young people with a lot of energy.  They learned that Sammie was a screamer, most unusual in Micronesia where people live so close together in extended family groups, and Sammie was not one to hold back her emotions.  She was an enthusiastic woman and believed she was in a private area.  Because of the stifling heat and humidity, their house widows were always open, the binds pulled up to let in the breeze, and the lights off.  But during the glow from a full moon at certain times of the month, the peeping lads were treated to a shadowy view of bodies bouncing up and down, and rolling around on the bed.  The gasping, screaming noises inside the house usually lasted for about an hour and some nights there would be a repeat performance.

Every night, the lads enjoyed this clandestine adventure, and often brought along drinks and snacks, kind of like watching an outdoor movie or going to a beach concert.  Their little group doubled in size.  The lads couldn't stop talking about the nightly episodes and the word soon got out.  Before long the local ladies heard about it and started to join in with their men in the jungle-watching area.  Sammie was obviously the center of attention until the ladies critiqued the show.  Roy's attention value tripled in a short time.  The ladies figured if Sammie screamed every night, then Roy must be an expert in the bedroom.  It was exciting to listen and watch.  It was rumored that several babies were conceived in the jungle after Sammie and Roy stopped for the night and fell asleep. The jungle observers got into the act.

Sammie and Roy were elated that everyone was friendly to them on the town streets and at the post office, and they got invited to all the important parties and barbeques. Several of the local ladies were noticeably flirting with Roy. They seemed to watch his tongue and lips very closely. For him, this was a reversal of roles. Sammie was usually the one getting the attention. Sadly, this new-found celebrity status only lasted a few more weeks for Roy.

As with most good things, loose gossip got the best of secrecy, and the news soon spread to various groups following the Sunday church service. Sammie's friend, Lucy Ragamar, heard the story, and told Sammy and Roy right away. Roy agreed with Sammie that they only had two choices, either be quiet during love making, or move to a concrete, air-conditioned building. Sammie guffawed and said that she couldn't give up her enthusiasm. That very night, the couple moved into a new concrete hotel with double-thick curtains and sound-proof walls. Several people gathered in the shadows near the hotel but to no avail. It remained graveyard quiet.

I talked to Roy next morning on the hotel veranda. They were happy with their new quarters and asserted, "I was getting real tired of those hungry jungle mosquitoes biting my butt and other private areas."

"How about the screaming? No problems?"

He laughed, "Damn exciting, Mon! Her screams bounce off the concrete walls three or four times in rapid succession. Talk about a crescendo finish!"

Sammie came sauntering out, eyes barely open, and headed for our table. She exclaimed, "Coffee, I need hot, black coffee!" Her voice was still raspy and dry from her nocturnal enthusiasm and the night's gymnastics.

# 15

# LEFTOVER JAPANESE MUNITIONS

There are still tons of munitions on the Micronesian Islands leftover from World War II (bombs, grenades, mortars, bullets). Micronesia was administered by the Japanese from about 1915 to 1945 and their army was well dug-in, preparing to fight the fast-moving American Army, aiming to reclaim the land for the local peoples. Some of the munitions were buried and hidden in caves, and some was simply plowed under at the end of the war. When the US decided to bypass heavily fortified Pohnpei on the path to the Philippines, Japan never had a chance to shoot at anyone and use the munitions. In fact, the military contingent on Pohnpei eventually surrendered about nine days (September 11, 1945) after the formal surrender by Japan on the USS Missouri (September 2, 1945).

Many new island construction projects currently result in the recovery of munitions, some American dude bombs but mostly hidden or discarded Japanese war materials. These fragile, unpredictable munitions are supposed to be carefully handled and made ready for disposal by the Naval Ordinance Units from Guam. The Navy does local trainings in English and island languages and explains how the munitions should be processed and made harmless. They assert continuously about how dangerous the munitions can be after rusting out and sitting in dirt and water. Obviously many people miss the trainings and the announcements, or are simply careless, or perhaps stupid.

As Pohnpei's National Capitol was being constructed on a former Japanese airfield, over three hundred Japanese mortars and thousands of rounds of ammunition were discovered. The police responded in beat-up pickups and showed no concern about the ordinance exploding. One of the older officers was overheard saying, "This stuff has been under water and it's all rusty. It's not going to explode." The police loaded the munitions onto the pickup and over bumpy deeply rutted gravel roads took their dangerous cargo to the police station. They casually stacked up the mortars like a cord of firewood next to the Police chief's office and not far from the officers' briefing and training room.

Carlos and I decided to stop in and visit with the chief, and explain what we were doing on the islands and who we were searching for. He was an old police and fire veteran, probably ready to retire, but still coherent and connected high in the island caste system. His name was Odoshi Fernandez, relating well in name and appearance to the two former colonial powers. As we walked into his office, we noticed all the munitions stacked outside his side window.

After we shook hands, I mentioned all the mortars leaning against a wall. I asked the chief if he was in contact with the Navy's Disposal Unit.

He answered, "One of my men has been trying for several weeks to get hold of those guys on Guam, but no luck."

Carlos said, "Chief, that ordinance is unpredictable. It could go off at any time."

"Even with all the rust? Hell, it's been sitting out in the rain for over a month. The ignition devices are probably dissolved."

Carlos grimaced.

I said, "Mind if I call the disposal guys? We need to get their opinion and maybe get the ordinance out of here."

The navy chief on Guam expressed his grave concern and said to cordon off the area pronto. I said that we were only visitors and handed the phone to Chief Fernandez. He kept nodding his head, with his forehead showing more worry furrows by the second. He ended by saying, "Okay, we'll do it. Yes, I understand."

The police chief had the nearby police offices evacuated and the area was roped off with yellow emergency tape. Ten sailors of the Navy Unit showed up two days later in a special transport plane. After inspecting the pile of mortars and ammunition, the navy officer directed the police and navy crew to professionally remove the mortars and transport the pile slowly in a padded truck to a selected disposal site. Other island munitions discovered previously were added to the pile for disposal. The combined load was then exploded through their explosive techniques and special devices. The explosions could be heard over the entire island. Shrapnel flew in every direction but because of proper safety planning, no one was injured. Two nearby coconut palm trees and a pandamus tree took direct hits and the fronds and branches nearly disintegrated.

Regarding the stack of mortars, it was never determined if some of the police officers were just careless or had a grudge against the chief and wanted to blow him up. When the navy instructors checked their records, it showed that most of the police officers and the chief had skipped the two previous trainings. The potential of a high-casualty situation had enough of a personal emotional impact that Chief Fernandez decided to retire and tend to his outlying farm. He passed his badge to a young, hard-charger who had been to the mainland colleges and had never missed a navy explosives training. It didn't hurt that the young man was related to the nanikin (royal prince).

Being that all of us were police retirees, a week later Carlos and I grabbed a case of soda pops and fruit drinks, with fresh sushi and tuna sashimi, and paid the chief a visit on his farm. He was wearing zories and shorts, looking ten years younger, and busily slopping his pigs. When he saw us, he motioned us to a homemade table under a giant avocado tree. It was shady and cool. His wife joined us an hour later with a huge bowl of fresh cucumbers, tomatoes, kamote, kancun, and course, avocadoes fresh picked from the tree.

Joking and laughing, we told our "war stories", added a little papalatong here and there, and related to one another like all cops do all over the world... a special bond; or maybe it was like that with all "older folks," reliving the glory days of youth. It was a satisfying, feel-good afternoon.

The chief had no idea where the missing governor might be, but added, "I've heard people have seen him down at the public market…"

# 16

---

# LEFT TO FEND FOR HERSELF

Through the island gossip at the pubic market and bar chatter, we heard that the missing governor might have gone to join some distant relatives in Kosrae, known as "the Island of the Sleeping Lady," because of it's of its silhouette profile at twilight. Formerly Kusaie in Japanese times, it is now called Kosrae, a 42-square mile island and is the easternmost of the Caroline Islands. One of the Ponapeian cops put us in touch with Kosrae Police Officer Lera Moses by texting. We decided to take the 300-mile flight from Pohnpei in a missionary prop plane. As we flew over Kosrae, we saw the great stone city of ancient Insaru with its rock buildings and canals. Many hundreds of years ago, members of this island civilization canoed to Pohnpei with Chief Isokelekel and his 333 warriors and captured the city of Nan Madol on Pohnpei.

During more recent times, the infamous Pirate Bully Hayes anchored in Lelu Harbor but his ship Leonora was sunk by a storm in 1874. It is rumored that he buried a treasure box of money and jewels on Kosrae but none has ever been found. In World War II, the Japanese Forces used Kosrae as a communications center, and for ranching and agriculture. The Americans chose to strategically bypass the island, thus there was little military action on the island except for sporadic bombing.

As we touched down, I noticed a slender, uniformed officer waiting near the exit gate. When we walked into the main terminal, she approached us and introduced herself. There was no mistaking me. I was easy to find being the only Caucasian, in a sea of happy, brown faces with bright, white teeth. Being Chuukese, Jorge didn't understand the local language. Kosrae has been isolated so long in history that their language is unrelated to other languages and patterns on the planet.

The officer was Lera Moses; and her uniform and appearance were immaculate and military precise. She was beautiful with a radiant smile, her skin shiny and chestnut brown, and features stereotypically Southseas, like a tropical Paul Gauguin painting.

She got us settled in at the Sandy Beach Hotel, and there we met for an early, leisurely dinner of fresh fish, lobster, taro, and variety of tropical fruits. She had put out her feelers for the missing governor with no luck. She said that most of the Kosraeans would know right away if someone from Saipan was visiting. She offered to drive us around the next day to make our own inquiries.

Lera said that Kosrae is mostly peaceful and religious, dating back to the Congregational church missionaries sailing from Hawaii to convert the non-believers. It had a very conservative beginning for traditional Christianity, and I noticed many of the women were wearing long "Mother Hubbard" dresses with flowery material with their arms and legs covered. Ler said that some of the modern girls were wearing shorts and tops with spaghetti dresses when they were off-island, but mostly they wore traditional clothing when at home. She said that it was expected if a boy and girl had sex, they had to confess to their parents right away and a hasty wedding would be arranged.

After a few wines and because we were outsiders, Lera spoke freely about her sexual orientation and said that she and another woman had been living quietly together for three years. They never flaunted their lesbianism, no one bothered them, and they each had a role – the other woman was the "housewife", and she was the provider, and as she proudly declared, "I'm the one that brings home the rice and chicken."

She shared some wonderful stories of her career, including stories about drunks, lunatics and fraudulent schemes gone bad. Carlos asked, "Do you remember some of your rookie days?"

She laughed and said, "I hope you guys are patient. This will take some time." She paused and looked at our Chuukese amigo, "Jorge will be able to relate to a lot of this."

I said, "Go ahead. Let's hear your history."

She started, "I always wanted to be a police officer. I studied criminal justice on the mainland, but had to come back before I received my degree because I ran out of money, and the island scholarship funds were all gone. I later learned the money had been reprogrammed to buy a car for one of the chiefs. Since there are no requirements to be a police officer and I came from one of the prominent families, I got a job right away and was assigned to an experienced officer, Jolly, for training. He tried to get me some handcuffs, but the pair we found were rusted closed, so we had to soak them overnight in paint thinner and later oil. We shared one common handcuff key. He checked me out a rusty revolver, but there was no ammunition for duty use or training. He found me a raggedy canvas holster that appeared to be left over from the Big War years."

Carlos laughed and said, "Great start. Anybody tell you about the laws and citizen rights?"

"Jolly tried to cover what he knew but he had started the same way I did...no formal training and no in-service. Some of what I learned was good, some very bad, and no one, including the supervisors ever on touched on communications or officer survival. Jolly is a good man, and the training went smoothly. Since I had been to college, I did most of the report writing, not only for our team but for others also. We made routine arrests but because of Jolly's physical size and deportment, we never had to use any force to make our arrests."

Carlos asserted, "Sooner or later, you were bound to run into a jerk who was drunk and wanted to fight."

"Oh yeah! It happened in my third week. We received a call about a bar fight at Panuelo's Bar, which is one of the few places where young people congregate and can sneak a drink or two. Jolly explained that we just had to separate the jerks, calm them down, and then send them separately on their way. However, when we rolled up in the Department's police truck, we were met with a barrage of rocks, chunks of concrete, and bottles. It looked like there were about thirty people fighting with each other, but when they saw us, their attention centered on us. It was a mini-riot just like you see on television."

"We had stopped the truck about thirty feet from the brawl and had exited. When the missiles started slamming against the truck, we ran to the opposite side of the truck. As Jolly slid back into the driver's side of the truck, he yelled, 'Lera, we gotta get out of here. Jump in the bed of the truck!' But I didn't hear him over the noise of the riot, and Jolly drove off with me standing in front of the mob without any protection. I yelled something like "shit," and ran like hell into the dark jungle. All I remember after that was rocks and bottles flying through the bushes and trees and narrowly missing me. Fortunately, there were no gunshots, and none of the rioters had the inclination or strength to follow after me."

I asked, "How did you find your way to the station?"

"Somehow, I got back to the station, all beat-up, bruised and with my uniforms in taters. The station was empty except for the janitor. He told me that everyone had bailed out of the station and headed to help Jolly and me after they heard his radio message calling for assistance. Once the responding officers got the riot calmed down, the search began for me. Jolly thought I had jumped into the truck and was really alarmed when they couldn't find me. The officers arrested a dozen people. It all ended up okay when they saw me back at the station. Jolly was apologetic and wanted to take on some of the rioters one-on-one; but I bought him a soda pop and got him to relax."

"What's your plans now?"

"Carlos, the family put the squeeze on all my cousins and uncles and got some money together, and it looks like I'm going back to college in Hawaii in just a few months."

"Trying criminal justice again?"

"My father put one proviso on the college money, that I would study sales, land management or any kind of business program. He doesn't want his oldest daughter to be dodging rocks and bottles."

I asked, "Is that okay with you?"

"Tom, I'll miss the friendships and the adrenaline rush, but not the flying missiles and drunks. Yeah, it's fine with me."

"What about your partner?"

"She's got a little money saved for her flight ticket. She's not interested in college, so once we get there, she'll be able to find a job. She's smart and quick, and a good worker." Micronesians are allowed to work in Hawaii through the agreements in the Compact of Free Association with the islanders.

Next morning we met with Lera and drove the island searching for tips about the missing governor. No luck, not even a hint of any type of rumor or possibility. We decided to stay one more night and leave the next morning.

During the evening, I stopped and talked to Evelyn, the local owner and manager of the hotel. We talked "hotels" and problems with shipments and employees, and I invited her up to the Beach Hotel on Saipan.

I had noticed an older man sitting under the palm trees with his laptop typing for hours at a time. Evelyn told me his name was Jack Withers, and that he was a detective story writer from New York, and liked to escape to the islands during the cold northeast winters from his home in Maine. He stayed in touch with his agent and publisher by email, and occasionally had to travel to New York to keep his contacts alive, and to keep the money flowing so he could afford to live in paradise.

Jack was a tall fellow with a full head of brown wavy hair and physically fit for his age, which I guessed to be about sixty. I noticed that two beautiful Japanese ladies, barely out of their teens, sat next to him, one on either side. I had seen them earlier getting off the dive boat. Jack ordered up some umbrella drinks and soon the threesome were laughing and hugging. He handed each of them a signed copy of one of his books. I strolled over to the group, introduced myself and learned that the ladies were Masako and Kenai, and they were on a month's diving tour of the Pacific. The ladies ordered up a large bottle of Tokyo sake and an appetizer of sashimi and sake, and some delicious rice cakes.

About an hour later, Kenai excused herself and said that she had to go pack for the next day's leg of their trip to Fiji. Jack and Masako decided to take a walk along the beach. I sat for a while enjoying my Filipino cigar and the last of the sake, and then decided to walk to a bluff overlooking the ocean, and watch the sunset. When I reached the top, I looked over the edge and saw that Jack was, as Elvis would say TCB, "taking care of business." He had Masako bent over a driftwood log facing the sea and both were enjoying the moments of ecstasy on a tropical beach. I couldn't hear them over the rush of the surf, but Masako's mouth was wide-open, like she was screaming at the setting sun. I left without being seen, and thought repeatedly of my warm, wonderful Cocina back home on Saipan.

While reading in my cabana, I heard Jack and Masako talking outside, and then looking through my bamboo blinds, I saw Masako leave for her room, and Jack knocking softly on Kenai's door. The lights went out in seconds. Next morning, both she and he, freshly showered, were late for breakfast. Jack and Kenai sat with Masako, and all three were full of smiles and acting giddy, faces flushed. Several of the regular patrons were grinning at Jack, and two of the guys shook his hand after breakfast.

Never being bashful, I asked one of the Japanese-speaking waiters what all the grinning was about. He replied, "When the Japanese girls came in for breakfast, Masako told Kenai in Japanese that Jack was a powerful lover and about being bent over a log on the beach. The girls forgot that Kosrae was a Japanese colony for about thirty-five years and many of the older people still know the language. Kenai then told Masako, 'I know about his power. For an old man, he can really fuck hard. He fucked me all night!' Then the girls started giggling. When they patted Jack on his legs, he started laughing with them."

I said, "So all the Japanese speakers know about Jack and his prowess?"

The waiter replied, "Even if Jack doesn't want it, he is now part of island legend and folklore. The story will be retold many times and before long, the number of satisfied females will be multiplied tenfold."

An hour later, we were saying goodbye to Officer Lera Moses and Kosrae. Jack had come to the airport to wish us well, and to give his Japanese ladies a sayonara hug. Our little investigations group was bound again for Pohnpei to hopefully to find some clues to help us find the missing governor on some other island. Masako and Kenai were off mentally on their next adventure, busily studying their maps, and maybe clandestinely thinking about another romantic interlude.

When we looked down at the lagoon from the plane, Jack was already walking along the beach, laptop over his shoulder, probably thinking about "who murdered whom" for his next mystery. He took timeout to make a long-sweeping wave up to us. I think he was smiling.

Kenai put down the map and released a long sigh downward. She half-heartedly managed a little wave through the window. As French lovers say, *que sera sera*.

# 17

**FINALLY, WORKABLE INFORMATION**

Captain Yancey Hilton and his woman Sally were waiting for us at the airport. He explained that the German ship guests wanted to explore and dive near the Nan Madol ruins. They planned to take the ship away for three days. Jorge asserted that they had to get permission from the local families, and probably pay three dollars per person to dive in the area. Yancey said that he had already met with the Madolenihmw Nahnmwarki (province high chief) of the area, paid him fifty dollars and won approval. Because Sally was a local islander, he tried to give her back change. Sally bowed and respectfully said, "It's for the family. Please keep it."

Yancey added that the chief kept the money and gave them an extra day for exploring and diving if they needed it. The dive time frame fit our schedule without a hitch.

Jorge wandered off to Sokehs Island where there is a large Chuukese population. He had several nosy aunties in the villages along the lagoon and figured if the governor had been in that part of Pohnpei, he would soon have the details. Being a smart nephew, he took along a fifty pound bag of California rice and a box of frozen square chickens imported from Louisiana. He was sure to be invited to a lot of homes.

Carlos and I drove to the public market to buy a freshly-caught yellow fin tuna and veggies for an early dinner. We spotted the national president's secretary, Maggie, across the aisles, about the same time she shouted Kaselehlia to us. She was a large, flamboyant woman with every female asset accentuated in size and proportion. She was loud and enthusiastic about everything she did. Her breasts were humongous, and caught the eye of every male in the marketplace. We had met her previously while introducing ourselves in the main government offices.

Maggie said she and her friends were going to a sakau bar that night and invited us to go along. Carlos had told me about the sakau bars, and we had heard the rhythmatic pounding of the pepper shrub root on basalt flat rocks as we had wandered along the trails. The juice is extracted from the root and combined with fresh water and then filtered through hibiscus fibers. A mildly narcotic, anesthetizing drink is produced and drank from a coconut half-shell. Locals and tourists alike compare the intoxicating ingredients to Fijian kava, but all share the opinion that the Ponapeian mixture is much stronger.

We agreed to meet Maggie that evening in the "Walk-in---Crawl-out Bar." The name alone showed great promise, especially after Maggie said to bring along some tobacco to chew and some beer to wash down the magic recipe. Carlos just shook his head, and said, "Another night to remember…if we can."

At the suggestion of several policemen, we drove out to the state capitol Palikir and spoke to about ten outer islanders, who had come ashore to escape several recent tremendous storms. With global warming and the glacier ice melting, some of the residents on lower atoll-type islands were in peril during high seas. We chatted with a dozen families with negative results about the missing governor. No immediate news but the request would travel fast from village to village.

On the way back to Kolonia, there was a public radio announcement from the medical board asking the betel nut chewers to stop 'eating the hospital." The betel nut concoction requires a nut, a pepper leave to hold the wad, some lime from ground-up coral, and some times the user adds a cigarette to add a jolt of nicotine. The chemical result of mixing with saliva is a red-colored, foul tasting and smelling substance with a slight buzz. The recent storms meant no boats could go out to fetch coral for their chew. Concrete on most of the Micronesian Islands is mixed with coral sand. The chewers knew this and simply knocked off pieces of the hospital walls, and ground it into lime powder for their chews. Several police officers noticed this, and rather than stopping the vandalism, joined in and made their own lime powder.

As we drove by the hospital, we observed that the radio announcement seemed to have little impact on the chipping. Carlos reflected, "It's loco for sure but maybe it's better to chip on concrete than to go out and break up the ancient coral reefs. If the sea settles down tomorrow, the lime suppliers will all be there with their hammers and baskets."

I asserted, "This is one substance-abuse island – sakau, tobacco, alcohol, marijuana and betel nut. I wonder if anyone here is really sober?"

Carlos said philosophically, "Not our worry unless they're driving cars and trucks. Let's go find Maggie and try out the sakau."

"Bless the hotel for sending a driver for us later."

We found Maggie and three of her lady friends right on time in the bar nahs (hut) in back. Two of the ladies were Ponapeian school teachers, and the other woman, Lexy, was a business consultant from the Solomon Islands. Maggie made a point of letting us know that they were all single. I said, whispering to Carlos, "Glad we're wearing our wedding rings. Should be a challenge of morality and monogamy after we get puputa (high) on sakau and beer."

Carlos smiled, "Not to worry, Amigo. There's plenty of guys here for the ladies. We'll have some fun, do a little flirting, and after we explain about Daisy and Cocina, they'll drift off to the other dudes. That's the way of the islands – very relaxed and low-key."

"That sensuous lady from the Solomons will require some willpower... the one with the humongous breasts and the flashing, chocolate-brown eyes."

"No problem, Tom. Just imagine she has five bratty kids and a bloodthirsty husband."

"That oughta do it, and add Cocina with her big, old axe."

Maggie listened in and asked, "You don't want Sexy Lexy?"

I stuttered a foolish answer, "Not the issue – I'm trying to be a good boy."

"I'm proud of you, but it's gotta be lonely with just Five-Fingered Mary."

Carlos and I both chuckled feebly.

Two hot, sweaty young men were pounding out the pepper root into a pulpy mess. I noticed that the water used in the juice was dipped from an old paint buckets loaded up from the nearby streams; and there were still wads of dirt stuck to the roots. After the filtering through a dirty rag, we were offered a cup each at the bargain rate of twenty-five cents each. I thought to myself, "Where else in the world can you buy dope for a quarter." The juice had the color of grey mud and a taste that could only be described as a blend of natural wood, chalk and a touch of dirt. After getting past the gag reflex, and downing a few cups, my head was reasonably coherent, but the knees felt detached and my lips numb.

Maggie became even more loud and boisterous, but in a very friendly, relaxed way. This is the stage that drunks go through and find it's mandatory to tell everyone how much they love them. She was a little more explicit and erotic, and declared, "This is when I give the best blowjobs of all. My inhibitions are totally gone, the lips are numb, and I feel hot all over. I want something that most girls never even think about. I like two cocks in my mouth at the same time and I like the high-protein juice." She stared intensely at Carlos and me, as much to say, "How about it?" She moved into our personal space.

Carlos was temporarily shocked and when he backed away from Maggie, he almost slid off the back of the wooden bench. I don't ever remember "Mr. Cool" losing his composure so quickly. I laughed and asked, "Time to talk about Daisy and Cocina?"

Gasping, he said, "Yep, right away. There's plenty of guys that will go for it."

I explained to Maggie about our married situation and wished her well. She slurred that she was disappointed and playfully grabbed my semi-erect interested soldier. She said that she had never had a white cock and a brown cock at the same time, only all the same color every time. She eyeballed a couple of tattooed California surfers a few tables over. She smiled, turned to me, and gave me an open, wet kiss on my numbed-out lips.

Maggie walked away, sashaying her ample hips distinctly from side-to-side. She was a lot of woman.

Carlos asked, "Feel anything, like past the warm drool?"

"Not much different than coming out from the dentist after a shot of Novocain."

As we accepted our third cup of sakau, a handsome young local man sat down next to us. He asked, "How could you turn down a blowjob from Maggie? Are you guys a couple?"

I said, pseudo cocky-like "Yeah, we're a couple, a couple of wise guys, tough guys…you get my drift? If you're looking for a fight, you'll have to wait until tomorrow. I'm not sure I can even stand up."

"In German, we refer to Maggie as *gutvik*. She's a good fuck!"

"Like I said, you can't get an argument or fight from us."

"No problem. I'm peaceful. My name is Rommy Weilbacher." He explained that he was a fourth generation mix of German ancestry and three to four different island groups. I noticed that he was dark mahogany like other islanders, but had a European nose, almost aquiline. He explained that half of his family is dark-skinned while the other half has Caucasian features and light skin. Even through the sakau haze, he got our full attention when he said, "I know where your missing governor is. Is there reward money for catching the guy?"

I asked, "If the information is right, you'll find yourself a few thousand dollars richer, some greenbacks for college. Can you take us to him?"

"*Schutzenfest* (piece of cake)! But first you have to talk to my father. He knows the location and the high-ranking family that owns the property."

We rounded up our hotel driver and off we went to the Village of Nett bouncing back and forth on dirt roads with potholes that could swallow a Volkswagen. When we drove up, Rommy's father, Henry, was fishing off the shore with a long bamboo pole. He was a huge man, probably over three hundred pounds and over six foot, six inches tall, obviously a lot of European stock in his genes. Rommy told us that his family was directly descended from the fierce fighters of the German colonist army *teufel hunden*.

Henry saw us and waved us over to a palm-thatched hut with a light bulb barely throwing out light. Moths as large as small birds were fluttering under the bulb. Rommy lit several foul-smelling mosquito coils to drive off the marauding insects.

After the introductions, Henry said that he knew where the missing governor was hiding, probably on the remote small islands of Ant Atoll, still in part of the State of Pohnpei. He said that Ignacio Antolin was not part of his extended family, and that the missing man was related to another clan in the bordering municipality of Kitti. Henry said that he would help out because he had heard over the coconut radio that Ignacio had stolen money from the common working people on Saipan. He added that some of the Ponapeian politicians were known to do the same.

We learned that Ahnt Atoll (commonly called Ant) is owned and controlled by the Napious Family, all descended from early European colonists and mixed with local residents. The family had carefully recorded their land holdings with the Spanish, German and Japanese colonial powers and there were no existing land disputes. Ant consists of thirteen low-lying, forested islets, about eight miles from Pohnpei, at 6"45'00" North, 158' East, with a total of about .72 square miles of land. Visitors are charged five to ten dollars per night to camp out. The Napious' owned Ant Atoll and hundreds of acres on the main island of Pohnpei. The administrator was Horatio Napious, and according to Henry and Rommy, an educated, intelligent man and probably reasonable to work out a solution in apprehending the wayward governor and returning the missing money.

Horatio was easy to locate. Besides being from a prominent family, he was also a successful businessman, dealing with the export of coconuts and fish. We found him in his air-conditioned office, feet up on his desk, and smoking the finest Philippines Cagayan cigar. When Carlos tried to explain the reason for our visit, Horatio said, "I already know everything about you guys, and what you're trying to do." The conversation was in English, the universal language of Micronesia. He continued, "I won't help you directly capture Ignacio; he's my distant cousin and our tradition stops me from putting a relative in jail on a crime of theft. If it was violence, I would walk along with you and bring him to justice."

I asked, "Horatio, what can you do then? How much can you help?"

He handed us cigars from a fresh box. "I'll give you a few free nights on the Ant Atoll, fill up some containers with fresh water, and maybe tell you where to rent a boat and captain. You already know he's there. He can't get off the Atoll area unless we go get him. He pays regularly for his transportation and supplies, and for renting a little shack on Nikalap Aku, the largest of the islets. We stay in touch by radio."

I said, "We won't need a boat and captain, just a guide. We have plenty of potable water. Our ship Shark Tooth should be back from Nan Madol today or tomorrow, and after loading on some fuel and provisions, we'll be ready to go."

"Should I let him know you're coming by radio?"

"Doesn't matter. He's not going anywhere. A call will get his mind and conscience into full throttle. That's good."

Carlos asked, "Is he armed?"

"He's an old out-of-shape man who's trying to live out his remaining days in peace and quiet. He's got a knife or two, and a spear gun, maybe a hatchet. He won't give you any trouble." He added, "But he's a stubborn old cuss. You'll probably have a tough time finding out where he stashed the millions."

Carlos smiled and declared, "Won't be a problem."

Horatio laughed and asked, "What are going to do…maybe beat the shit out of an old man to get your information?"

"No…just hold his head under water for about forty seconds. It's a fast way to find out if a man still wants to live." Carlos waved adios and left the room.

Horatio looked over at me with an inquisitive look.

I shrugged my shoulders and whispered, "He's a laugh a minute. I never know his next move."

"Hell, he could kill the old man."

I answered, "Ever look a Doberman straight in the eyes, with their irises going from side to side? Carlos is the same way. You know the canine is going to make a decisive move – you just don't what, but it will happen."

"Aieeee!"

# 18

## OFF TO AHNT ATOLL

As we reached the seaport, the Shark's Tooth was docking. When the tie-downs were secured, Yancey came bounding down the gangplank, followed by Sally. She was more beautiful and graceful than I remembered. Her light skin had taken on a golden tan, probably from all the sun exposure and diving at the ruins of Nan Madol. I realized once again that I had been away from Cocina much too long.

We filled Yancey in with the news about the governor and Ant Atoll. He was ecstatic, saying that was one island paradise that he had never visited. He added that his German guests would be excited and overwhelmed with this new adventure, the extra trip not being on the itinerary. The atoll was so remote that Sally had never been there but she had heard about the serenity and beauty of the islets, and that the lagoon was teeming with sea life, and that a modern Robinson Crusoe could easily survive if there was a way of catching and storing rain water.

We loaded up the ship with fresh water, provisions and fuel. Yancey planned on leaving early the next morning and by studying the charts, he figured we had about a three hour ride, maybe longer if the Germans decided to troll for barracuda and yahoo.

Yancey, Sally and the Germans opted to hit the sakau bars. Carlos and I took a pass, me in particular, knowing that Sexy Lexy, the business consultant from the Solomons, would even look even better than the night before, if that was possible. I took a cold shower, read a book and drifted off to sleep, intermittently thinking about how Lexy would look naked, and then dreaming about the family on Saipan. Carlos was too edgy to rest and did a two-hour workout on heavy weights at the outdoor jungle gym, and then a ten-mile run on the Awak Road. When he finally fell asleep, his snoring was probably irritating the chickens and night rodents a dozen miles away.

Next morning, Yancey and Sally looked alert and ready to sail. The three Germans were another matter. They were disheveled, flushed and wrinkled. They had paced themselves with the sakau and beer, but most definitely not with Maggie and her three friends. They had ended up some remote no-tell, short-time motel with the ladies and barely made it to the ship on time. They did not respond well to a hearty *guten morgen*.

Yancey had warned everyone before that the ship sails on schedule, and if you miss it, better charter a speedboat to catch up or rent a seaplane to meet up at the next port. It was a rough sea, with eight-foot rollers, and the weary, green-colored Germans decided not to fish enroute to the Atoll. All three of them sat on lounge chairs at the bow, sucking in fresh air, guzzling pints of water, and trying to regain their strength.

I glanced over at Carlos and said, "That could be us."

"Thank goodness for our wives. I never wanna feel that bad. The big blonde fellow has been "blowing chunks" ever since we left the harbor. Don't stand downwind."

As we neared the Tauenai Pass, the entrance to the Atoll, we were immediately surrounded by a school of spinner dolphins, maybe twenty, all playfully swimming around the ship, and then under, popping up on the opposite side. They were magnificent creatures and kept screaming at us in their animal language. Sally yelled back at them in a language that sounded eerily close to their own. Several of the dolphins actually paused, looked at her, and screeched back directly to her. We slowed to enter the narrow pass, and the dolphins decided to go play and hunt in the open sea.

It was high tide so the pass was easy to navigate. It was a novelty for the birds to see the Shark's Tooth, and we soon had noddies, terns and frigate birds flying near and over us. Yancey said that the birds believed us to be fishing vessel, and were waiting for the heads and entrails of our catch to be thrown overboard. As we circled the lagoon, we saw no signs of human life. There were no boats anchored inside the lagoon.

Horatio had told us that the best islet for camping was Patya, which had perfect beaches and large mangroves for shade when it was high noon and too hot to move about. We were only about six degrees above the equator. Yancey threw out the anchor, and lowered a dinghy for going back and forth from the ship to the shore. Sally had removed all her clothing except for a bikini bottom. She didn't bother with the dinghy, dove over the side and swam ashore.

Yancey saw us staring in disbelief. He declared, "She's a beautiful island girl if there was ever one. My nickname for her is the "Reef Girl." She's part of the earth and the sea, and can swim effortlessly along the reef for over sixty seconds underwater. By the way, the unwritten rule at remote atolls, is "clothing optional." She would be au naturel without her bikini if she knew you better. She doesn't want to be rude."

Carlos and I usually only wore our beach trunks on Saipan, and off came the clothes. We followed the lead of Yancey, and when he stripped down to the buff, we dropped our trunks. He smiled and said, "Keep in mind, you'll need your clothes when you're in the sun too long or when you're snorkeling; and then again, at night when the pesky gnats and mosquitoes decide to do their mischief." He paused, "And don't sit on any hot rocks or boards. You may burn "the boys" big-time."

The Germans still looked hung-over and bedazzled from the previous night, and this clothing thing was much too much for them to handle right away. They jumped onto the dinghy and rowed ashore. Yancey, Carlos and I dove over the side and swam to the pristine beach. The water was crystal clear. I figured the underwater visibility was one hundred feet or more. About eight five-foot reef sharks followed us in.

When we walked up onto the shore, Yancey said, "Don't worry about them. They're just young sharks, and they're curious. They want some handouts — just like the birds. If they get too close, just punch them in the snout. They'll go away."

I thought to myself, "What if we piss them off, and if they're five-foot long, where are their parents and how long are the hungry adults?"

Yancey good-naturedly replied, "Hell, just swim faster if you have to."

Sally had already found Ignacio's camp and his fire, and some pots and pans. She pointed out a near-by shack made from palm fronds and bamboo poles. He had apparently moved from Nikalap Aku and built another shack on Patya. There was a large barracuda cleaned and filleted on a makeshift table, and ready to be barbequed. Judging by a large hole just behind its head, it had apparently been expertly speared. She said that his food supply was safely secured in a huge waterproof container. He had been catching water from a large canvas that funneled the water into a fifty-gallon drum. Ignacio was nowhere to be found, and his spear gun and knives were missing.

Sally's breasts were standing proud, and I tried to keep my eyes at eye level. I noticed Carlos was looking away down the beach, likely to avoid being branded a pervert, and Yancey was smiling at our discomfort. He said, "Just relax. You'll get used to her…well, maybe. I never have. Every time I end up in one of these remote areas with her, I find myself falling back into heavy-duty lust and love. She's a raving beauty."

I hesitatingly replied, "Yeah, like maybe in the next lifetime."

Carlos asked, "Tom, what's the plan? Should we just wait him out? He's probably hiding in the brush or the mangroves."

"Yep, sounds like a good idea. We can have an early supper before it gets dark. Looks like we have a barracuda on the menu. Thanks to Ignacio."

Yancey, "He'll probably come out when he gets hungry, or the bugs will drive him out while they try to eat him a mini-chunk at a time." He added, "Everyone will have the option of living on the boat or camping out in the shack. It almost rains every night, so it will be damp for camping. The bugs won't be too bad - the shack is in a breeze open area near the water. Plus, we have some repellent and mosquito coils."

I said, "I often wonder what kind of chemical shit you're breathing in when you have the coils burning. If it chases away bugs, they can't be too healthy for your lungs."

Carlos replied, "I always try to read the ingredients on the package, but it's always in some Asian character writing. I try and avoid them whenever I can."

Sally already had a fire going and was cooking rice and vegetables. She told Yancy that there were some good coals for barbequing the fish. She had already made sashimi from the white belly of the barracuda which is considered a delicacy and an energy food for one's health. We were in for a delicious island banquet. Carlos rounded up some cold San Miguels and some diet sodas, and the Germans put some relaxing European music on the ghetto blaster. The orchestra sounds were clean and sharp as they echoed through the jungle.

I put new batteries in the bullhorn and announced to Ignacio in friendly terms that he should come in for a meal and talk to us. There was no reply and he hadn't shown by the time the sun was starting to set. Almost everyone decided to shower back on the ship and sleep in their nice comfy beds. The ship's crew had already built another hut for their nights on the island. They had plenty of cold beer. Sally fixed a meal for Ignacio and left it in on the table in a tightly sealed plastic container. Along with a flashlight, I left a note for Ignacio, explaining who we were and that we had no intention of leaving the lagoon until we had a face-to-face confab.

Next morning by the time most of us were awake, Sally had already swam ashore with a float carrying enough food for the next three meals. I could smell the coffee from the deck, and when I looked towards the fire about thirty yards away, I saw that Sally had decided to forego the bikini bottoms. She was as natural to the setting as the swaying palms and the blooming flowers. I could feel a primitive urging deep inside my guts.

Seeing Yancey snorkeling along side of the ship, I quickly brought myself back to reality. She was another man's woman. I had read about primitive circumstances, where a woman is isolated with a group of men, and that hot passions developed among the males, and murders took place. One of the best recent examples is the story of Kazuko Higa, a Japanese woman who was stranded on Anatahan Island, eighty miles north of Saipan, after her fishing boat was dive-bombed by American planes in 1944; and she was shipwrecked along with thirty military and civilian Japanese adult males. Before she and other survivors were rescued in 1951 by US Navy sailors, she had taken on at least four "husbands" and various "interlopers," and at least four of the males had been murdered. There were other mysterious deaths that were attributed to illness or drowning. On later interviews with the survivors, Kazuko was fully clothed most of the time and was not flirtatious. But her mere presence and raging hormones set off the male desires for coupling and propagation. It is generally recognized that Kazuko was not impregnated, but after the war when she returned to Japan, she learned that her legal husband had "declared her dead" and remarried. None of the island survivors were ever charged with murder.

Part of the returning reality was knowing that I would not be stranded on a remote island watching a beautiful naked woman that I couldn't touch, and that I would be back home with my precious Cocina within weeks. Kazuko and her "men" had an entirely different situation. For single, lonely men, six years is a long time without female companionship.

Yancey saw me looking down from the deck, and yelled, "Get your snorkeling gear. We'll take a look around. Sally will have breakfast ready in about twenty minutes."

I grabbed my mask and goggles and joined Yancey for a quick review of the day to come. The water was clear and refreshing, and I soon learned why Ant Atoll is one of the favorite places for experienced, well-traveled divers. There were coelenterates, coral polyps, sponges, giant clams, and colorful staghorn, fire and brain corals in abundance. The fish population was diverse with schools of jacks, barracudas, squid, and a hundred different kinds, sizes and colors of reef fish. It seemed like a giant, abundant-color aquarium, but in this case, it was nature in the wild at its best. I saw several reef sharks moving towards Yancey, and when one got too close, he punched it full on the nose. The shark swam away, along with his fellow predators.

I heard a bell ringing. As I stood up in the shallows, Sally was gesturing at us to come in for breakfast. She slipped back into her bikini bottoms. When I sat down at the rustic table, Sally showed me where Ignacio has snuck in during the night and carried away his supper that she had left out. There were footprints in the sand, probably about Ignacio's size, but there was a smaller set of prints, either a child or a woman. She said he had also taken several fruits and some of the sashimi. He also took the note and flashlight, and two of his blankets and a pillow from his shack.

I declared, "If he doesn't come in today, we just make a circular sweep around all the little islands of the lagoon. The islets are close together, and at low tide, you could walk to most of them."

Breakfast was scrumptious and even tasted better than on the ship, being prepared by Sally and eating and cooking in the open spaces. By noon, Sally had prepared a light meal, and the tide was moving out. Still no sign of Ignacio. I made several more announcements on the bullhorn.

Carlos asserted, "Let's do it. We'll make a sweep using the ship's crew on the southeast side, and you and I can go northeast, and then we'll all meet up on Bird Island. I'll get everyone together for a briefing and we'll make a plan."

Carlos got the crew organized in the shade under a huge pandamus tree. Yancey and Sally decided to stay behind and watch the ship, the lean-to shack and the food. I knew he wanted some private time, when he winked and said, "You never know. Ignacio might double-back or swim across the lagoon. Sally and I have to be on the look out for any of his shenanigans."

I returned his wink and smiled in amusement.

I advised the searchers that Ignacio was only wanted for a theft crime and he had never displayed any violence tendencies. Even though he had a spear gun and some knives, there was no expectation that he would attack, even if he was cornered up. Every searcher was carrying a machete, for self defense if needed, but mainly for cutting through the jungle. Carlos and I headed north.

In the first several hundred yards, we found several fresh footprints. The impressions then ended as we reached a smelly, mundungus billabong where the ocean seemed to come in and dump all its refuge. It was filled with ugly plastic bottles, feces from sea animals, strange-shaped fungi, a few old tires and a marine battery, and a large hunk of decaying flesh.

Carlos said, "About the right size for Ignacio. Could be him."

As we drew closer, we saw that it was an old grey-muzzled dolphin, which probably had come to a quiet place to rest at high tide, and then got caught when the tide subsided. The body was covered with flies, and rats scurried away as we got closer. Mother Nature was well into recycle.

We saw footprints through the muck on the other side of the swamp heading north. There was a smaller size next to the man's footprints. It was an easy trail to follow. We sensed a flash of light cross our eyes and saw that the ship's crew members were signaling us with a mirror from across the lagoon. They were also heading north and we would probably meet in about two hours, having completed the circle around the lagoon.

The inner lagoon area had beautiful, soft sand, but on the outside, it was open, rough ocean with rocks, broken coral and large trees, many of which had fallen into the ocean, likely during one of the last typhoons. As we waded across the water separating us from Bird Island, we saw the smoke from a fire near the shore on the sandy side. It was an older man, probably Ignacio, sitting on a piece of driftwood in front of the fire and staring into the flames. He appeared to be in a trance or half-asleep. He was wearing a wrap-around skirt. His spear gun and knives were atop a large piece of coral about ten yards away.

The sounds of our approach brought him into full consciousness. He glanced quickly at the spear gun and knives, but when he saw the goliath bulk of Carlos, I could tell by his body language that he gave up the idea of arming himself. We approached within ten feet. I introduced myself and then Carlos.

He said, "I read your note. I figured someone would be searching for me but not this soon. I left a trail of hotels and car rentals all over Florida and Europe, thinking the FBI or some other government agency would spend a couple of years bogged down in those areas. A few million dollars doesn't mean much to the Feds."

Carlos asserted, "Well, we're here now." Not one to hesitate and knowing the money that was stolen belonged to his island of Saipan, he continued, "We just want to get the fucking money back to the people, and we'll be on our way. I don't care what happens to you. You're just a bag of basura."

Ignacio didn't respond and looked down into the sand. He mumbled something about we didn't have jurisdiction or authority.

Carlos slapped him on the back of the head and declared, "Asshole, we are out in the middle of the Pacific. Where's your stupid brain? There's no fucking courts or rules. It's like Darwin wrote about the survival of the fittest, and right now we are the fittest and the strongest.

We could throw you in the billabong and no one would ever know. The rats would eat you up in a week."

I put my arm on Carlos' back to calm him down. He was well into his crazy-man act. I asked, "Ignacio, where's the other person…the smaller one that was with you?"

He yelled towards the jungle, "Sawanawan, you can come out now."

A young woman, probably about seventeen, wearing only a turquoise sarong around her waist, came walking towards us from the mangrove trees. Her breasts were ample and fully developed. She was absolutely gorgeous, again another stereotypical female that you might see on a tourist brochure about the Pacific islands. Her abdomen was protruding, her body appearing to be about four months pregnant. She nodded a greeting.

Without hesitating, Ignacio explained, "Sawanawan is my niece many times removed in our family history. She was sent with me about five months ago by her family to take care of me."

Carlos said, "The family probably meant cooking and fishing, not impregnating the young girl."

"I'm not making excuses. One thing led to another. She had never had sex and wanted to learn. I was getting lonely for my wife. I also had a mistress from the Philippines that no one knew about. I would visit her in Manila every month or so, on my business trips. I miss having a woman close by."

Carlos asked, "So why did you get the girl pregnant? It's appears too late for an abortion. You've really screwed up her young life, especially when the family finds out and everyone is going to be embarrassed and shamed. Sex with someone in your own clan is taboo."

"No drug stores for condoms." It was a very feeble attempt at a joke. He shrugged his shoulders.

"Fuck you, asshole. If I were her father, I'd cut off your gonads and feed them to the sharks."

I asserted, "We have the money to consider, but also how to get the girl some medical attention. She's young and it's her first baby. She's going to need good nutrition and vitamins, and a physician. She won't get that out here."

Carlos said, "I think we can easily solve the medical problem. She's a Micronesian so she can travel to Saipan through Guam, and we can hook her up with a good doctor. Besides when we get the money back from this piece of shit, we can use some for her medical costs. After she delivers, she can work the situation out with her family, or even put the baby up for adoption."

Ignacio said that the girl spoke rudimentary English. I asked Sawanawan if she understood and if she wanted to go to Saipan. She looked over at Ignacio, who nodded his approval and tried to force a smile. She did not respond.

The ship's crew had met up with us. I asked the chief mate to take the girl back to Sally. Without a word, Sawanawan stood up and walked towards the ship. She never looked back at Ignacio. I wrote a quick note to Sally, asking her to fix the girl up with plenty of good food and a bed on the ship, and gave it to the chief mate. Carlos also gave Ignacio's spear gun and knives to carry back to camp.

It was time to deal seriously with Ignacio. I did not see a happy ending any time soon.

# 19

## FINDING THE MILLIONS

Ignacio sat quietly, still staring into the sand.

I declared, "Ignacio, I'm going to teach you about astringency. You politicians hate the word and the circumstances."

"What the fuck is astringency."

I smiled, "See, I knew you wouldn't know that word or concept. Simply put astringency is telling people what they don't wanna hear and leading them to where they don't wanna go. It's not comforting them about their current situation, like between a rock and hard place, or reassuring them things will get better. In plain talk, your situation is likely to get worse and only you can determine how soon it will start getting better."

He frowned and said, "I don't know what the hell you're talking about."

I said, "Okay, Ignacio. How do you want to do this? Tell us where to find the money, and once we get it, you're a free man...or we can haul your butt back and turn you over to the FBI, and let you deal with federal charges. The local cops will be charging you with statutory rape. You'll get so much time in prison, that you'll never see or feel the ocean again, except in your dreams...or nightmares."

"Don't try to intimidate me. I've been threatened a dozen times and I'm still alive and ticking. I don't know where the money is, and that's final."

I glanced at Carlos. I knew that he wanted ten minutes alone with this stubborn old man, and answers would come flying out. That's always a problem when you use torture, the subject will blurt out whatever he can think about – might be false but at least he gets the pain to stop. I said, "Carlos, throw your cuffs on this jerk, and we'll start back to camp. Put the cuffs in front and he start acting up, cuff him behind his back."

Surprised, Ignacio said, "We're not going to talk anymore?"

"Why? You said that you didn't know where the money was, so why keep talking. We're going to take you back to our camp, and chain you to a coconut tree until we're ready to sail. You might as well get used to being chained up. No more freedom for you. Take a mental picture of the atoll – you'll going to die in prison and never see the ocean again." Ignacio seemed further surprised and was now alarmed with his eyes open wide, nostrils flaring, obviously moving into a full-blown panic attack. Being chained to a tree is a long way down from being a hotshot governor of a small commonwealth.

"You can't do that to me. You just can't take a human being and chain him like a dog. I'll call the FBI and I'll file a civil rights violation."

"Good, we can file our complaints together. We'll sail direct for Guam where the main FBI office is located." Carlos was standing behind Ignacio and was sporting an ear-to-ear grin. I could see that he was happy with my tact. I was tackling Ignacio's ego straight-on and blasting the crap out of the self-image of his own importance.

Carlos slapped Ignacio again on the back of his head and asserted, "While you're with the FBI, you can also file a complaint on me for police brutality." He wrapped his huge hand around the back of Ignacio's neck, pulled him to his feet, and said, "Let's go. Your dog chain awaits. We'll have to come up with a special doggie name just for you…maybe 'Pukey.' Yeah, I like that."

Carlos slipped a rope through the handcuffs, and walked Ignacio like an animal on a long leash. Every time Ignacio jerked on the rope,

Carlos pulled harder, causing Ignacio to fall on his face several times in the soft, wet sand. Carlos looked at me and said, "Slow learner."

I smiled and nodded in the affirmative.

Just before we got back to camp and within earshot of his prisoner, Carlos asked to be alone with Ignacio. He exclaimed, "A few minutes will this turd will get all the information we need."

I answered, "Not yet. Maybe later if he decides to be stubborn and foolish." I pointed to a coconut tree with very little shade, and said, "Just tie him to the trunk. We might bring him food and water, but maybe not."

Ignacio yelled, "You can't treat me like this. I'm still the governor, and I've got connections. The Feds will be all over your butts."

Ignacio continued to rant and rave but after several hours with the sun at full center overhead, the heat finally calmed him down, and he retreated into the shade that the coconut tree slightly provided. Within several hours, he had lost his high and mighty demeanor and meekly asked for water.

When the sun faded into the horizon, Sally brought him a plate a food and a gallon of water. She didn't speak to him. He said, "Woman, you gotta help me. This isn't right that Parker and Carlos treat me this way. I'm the governor and the elected authority of the Marianas Islands. I'm your elder."

Sally stared at him and still didn't speak.

He stood up and demanded, "I have to go to the toilet. Untie me so I can go back in the jungle."

Again, she didn't speak, until he continued to be demanding and loud. She looked him directly in his eyes, "Dig a hole, you fucking bastard!" She spat in the sand, turned her back and walked back to the beach.

She heard the buzz of mosquitoes as they were preparing and swarming for their new tasty morsel. Sunset is their favorite feeding time.

# 20

---

# FULL DISCLOSURE

For the next two days, we continued to snorkel and dive and explore most of the lagoon. We were in no hurry, accomplishing our main mission of finding the governor. Sally continued to fill the pregnant teenager with fruits and veggies, and multiple vitamins. Sally had been around pregnant relatives many times on the islands and had experienced native midwifery training. She examined the young girl and pronounced her healthy and strong. There was no hurry to rush back to a doctor and hospital on Pohnpei.

Ignacio continued to live under his coconut tree, moving ever so slightly to try and stay in the tree's skinny shadow. Out of her humanity, Sally kept him provided with food and water, and found an old straw hat to keep him from burning up in the sun. She didn't talk to him or show him any sympathy. Her dealings with the man were all business.

Finally on the third day, Carlos strolled over to Ignacio's tree and asked him if he was willing to talk about the missing money. Ignacio's only response was whining and complaining about his treatment. Carlos went closer and slapped him on the back of the head. He asserted, "Get straight with us, you asshole. You took our people's money and we want it back for the old people's medical care and some for the children's education. Shit, when Tom's out fishing, I might just come back and beat the truth out of your sorry ass."

Ignacio stared at the sand.

Sally didn't come with his dinner that night, only a bottle of warm water. She said, "Carlos told me to just to give you water. You can live a long time without food."

He demanded, "Tell Tom Parker to get over here. I want him to know about Carlos and all this bullshit. This is abusive behavior."

Sally answered, "Tom and Carlos are out fishing right now with Yancey. He knows about no food and just water for dinner. Yancey even said that you're too fat and that a stringent diet would be good for your health."

"I'm going to let all the authorities know about this treatment. You people are crazy. You'll all go to jail."

"And how are you going to do that, Silly Man. You got an army? You don't even have a jungle drum, let along a cell phone. Go to sleep and think about telling the truth."

Ignacio started to mumble a profanity until Sally caught his eye. He stopped and looked away, common sense taking over. He knew she wouldn't hesitate to kick his ass.

Next morning, I took an egg burrito and a cup of coffee over to Ignacio. He gulped the burrito down without saying a word, and then slowly sipped on the coffee.

I asked, "Are you ready to talk about the money, or do you wanna spend the rest of your life in prison? It's kinda your call at this stage. Remember astringency? We're heaving anchor tomorrow and heading back to Pohnpei and then Guam."

"I don't wanna go to prison. Maybe we can work out a deal."

"A deal sounds good to me. What's making you hesitate in this whole thing? There's no way you'll be able to keep anything you own. You're caught and no more running. The Attorney General lawyers will sue for everything you own, right down to your wristwatch and underwear. They'll get everything your wife and daughter own too. Ask OJ what the lawyers can do."

"I want to leave my family some money to continue on. They can stay in California. I want to live my last days on a tropical island. The family likes the city and being close to hospitals, movie theaters, and shopping malls."

"Now you're getting reasonable. I was close to turning Carlos loose to get some answers. Yancey said I should so we can get this thing settled. We don't care about your worthless hide and throwing you in the bucket…but what we do care about is getting most of the money back to the Marianas Islands."

He grimaced, "Look I wanna leave my family with a million dollars and maybe I'll turn the rest over to you; but you gotta promise me 'no prison.' I would wither away behind bars."

"A million is too much…maybe about a fifth of that. That would be plenty to get your daughter through college, and then she can go to work like the rest of us. I can't make a promise about prison. That's up to the authorities, but there's no requirement that I turn you over to the police, or even take you back. My only job is to get the money back to the government."

He pleaded, "Give me three hundred thousand for the family and it's a deal. You probably already know about the fifty thousand I stashed in the Bank of Guam."

"Yep, it all works for me. Close enough. We already know about the nine hundred thousand dollars in the California bank, and there's a hold on most of the money. You can have the fifty thousand for your survival money. It's not going anywhere until we give our approval. But now, where's the big stash, and how do we access it? There should be about 3.5 million hidden somewhere."

Ignacio asked, "You did know about the fifty thousand on the Bank of Guam under my cousin's name, right?"

"I do now, and yeah, you can keep it for your future. You planned and worked hard. Maybe you're entitled to a small piece of the pie. But don't rationalize too much – you're still a thief and an embezzler."

Ignacio talked openly and freely with Carlos and me throughout the night. We took copious notes, made a few phone calls to California. The time and day difference was perfect. The banks were still open on the West Coast and most of my financial contacts were still in their offices.

Ignacio gave us all the account numbers and passwords. He had originally placed the money in a Greek offshore bank, moved it to Fiji, and the bucks were now in the Cayman Islands, but not for long. While sitting in the banks, it had gained over $100,000 in interest. I directed this additional income to Ignacio's family in California, and the balances appropriately divided into the Saipan government account, and of course, the Private Investigations Agency account.

Carlos later asked, "Why give the asshole anything? Fuck him... he doesn't deserve a nickel."

"Just a matter of honey and vinegar. We got what we want, and there's money for his family."

From the pristine Ant Atoll, we sailed for Pohnpei the next day, and once ashore, did some fine-tuning on the accounts. The Cayman Bank wanted additional identification information on Ignacio, so we fax'd them a set of his fingerprints and also his passport photo which he had used to start the account.

I could tell that Ignacio was getting jumpy and nervous about what would happen after we settled the accounts. He was torn between leaving right away back to Ant, or following my lead in firmly requesting that he stay with the Shark Tooth until we were sure the money was all squared away. I didn't want any more last minute hassles that only he could straighten out or give permission.

Once we got the tentative clearance from the Cayman Bank, we headed out to sea enroute to Guam. I assured Ignacio that he wasn't going to be arrested, at least on our information, and that everyone on Saipan had been told that he had simply disappeared again somewhere in the islands around Pohnpei and Kosrae.

Ignacio said, "Let me go now. You've got the clearance and the money will be transferred. Nothing to worry about. Tell them I disappeared at sea during a storm."

Carlos answered, "You're not going anywhere until we get the final approval. Calm down or I'll tie you up again."

"You young people have no respect."

Carlos smiled and said, "No need to argue with you, or try to set you straight, you dirtbag. You stole money from the kids and the old people *manamko*. Just be fucking quiet."

A day went by. The phone finally rang on the next afternoon. The money had cleared and it was now safely in the Saipan banks. We saw Ignacio listening from an open window. We all celebrated, including the German tourists who had become an informal part of the team. Sally and the ship's cook broke out some champagne and peppery hors de'oeuvres, and played some hot reggae music. The dancing began, along with sad attempts at karaoke. It had to be one of the worse gawd-awful contribution to the world by the Japanese.

Carlos went to check on Ignacio in his cabin to give him the good news and invite him for a drink. He was gone and so was his life vest. The ship's orange float ring was also missing. A thorough search just confirmed that Ignacio was not aboard. Everyone came up on deck. About three hundred yards, an orange float was spotted bobbing up and down over the waves. Yancey adjusted his binoculars and saw that Ignacio was swimming vigorously for Nowwin Atoll, the center of the Hall Islands.

Carlos asserted, "What the hell does he hope to do there, even if he makes it? He doesn't know the people or the language."

I said, "Who knows what was bubbling around in his mind. All I know is that he doesn't want to go back to civilization and face the charges. He really frightened about being locked up. He just wants to disappear on one of the tropical islands."

Yancey asked, "Should we go get him? The water's still deep there for the ship, and we can pick him up in about forty minutes."

Through the binoculars, I observed him swimming hard and struggling to find his freedom. "No, he called it. He's a grown man. He's knows what he wants to do." I gave him a half wave over the stern and said, "Let's stay on course for Guam. We'll re-confirm the money again before we give the final news to the Saipan Auditor."

# 21

## SWIMMING WITH THE MANTAS

I gave up thinking or worrying about Ignacio, or if he made it to shore. Jumping ship in the Hall Islands was his choice and in reality, he was mostly tired of living and just wanted to fade away on one of the islands. Maybe the sharks got him, or he was too weary to keep struggling and sunk deep onto the ocean floor. We'd know soon enough if he survived when we watched the Bank of Guam for his periodic withdrawals. The closest bank branch was in Moen and then if he got to the main island, he would probably make his way back to Pohnpei where he knew the language and had relatives. Maybe the war-like Chuukese would aerate with spears before he ever got to the airport.

Yancey and Sally said that they had special treat for us on Guam and what a major surprise it was. We were going swimming with the giant mantas off the shore of Tumon Bay at a secret spot that their friend Nicky Campos knew. They had heard Carlos and me talking about making a trip to Yap and Palau to take photos and study the giant manta rays (manta birostois). A little research showed that that they were colloquially known as "devilfish", and at maturity, measured 18 feet across their wing tips and could be up to 20 feet long, some record mantas weighing up to five thousand pounds.

We contacted several banks on Guam, confirming that the transfers of the "big" money to several accounts, including the Private

Investigations Agency account, was finished. The math was fundamental – 4.5 million dollars embezzled, $50K to Ignacio, $300,000K (we didn't count the interest) to his family in California, $40K spent by Ignacio while traveling around and bank fees, leaving a balance of $4,020,000, minus at 20% $804,000 for our fee, with $3,216,000 being returned to the government on Saipan. It was definitely a good day for our agency. The money was in all the accounts as directed. When I gave the balances to Carlos, he literally jumped for joy, grinning from ear-to-ear, and lighting up the universe with his white teeth. When Augie Garcia, the Saipan auditor, heard the final accounting, he screamed so loud that we probably didn't need a telephone to hear him all the way to Guam.

By two o'clock in the afternoon we were standing on the shoreline waiting for Nicky, snorkeling gear in tow. We looked down the beach and along came two tall hombres, one of whom was the Beach Hotel Tennis Pro Jonah. Jonah was a good friend and we were happy to find him on Guam. Nicky and Jonah were longtime compadres, and when Nicky heard about Yancey and Sally bringing us to his secret spot, he called Jonah, who hopped the next commuter prop plane and was soon ready to go exploring with us.

After introductions, Nicky explained that there was an opening in the reef about four hundred yards offshore. The mantas liked to ride the currents in and out of the bay and feed just before and during sunset. Nicky said that few people knew about the spot, and he made us stand in a circle, touch hands and vow that we would not tell other people about his "secret spot" except for very close compadres like ourselves. In jest, he then did some hocus-pocus mumbling about the gawd-given rights of "fish and sea creatures," and placed a curse on anyone who revealed the secret place.

Nicky said, "If you tell people about our secret spot, your karma will turn to shit, and unforgettable and unforgivable evil things will come into your life." Rightfully so, he was concerned that the area would be overrun with tourists and the fish would disappear because of all the noise and commotion. Ironically that is often the way – you want to share something spectacular with friends and family, and soon everything changes because the secret is out, and people can be thoughtless spoilers.

Nicky explained that the opening in the reef served many purposes. One of which were the natural breaks in the coral, known as cleaning stations, where the mantas could rest and the reef fish would come and clean the parasites off from their skin. The mantas also like to feed on the krill and planktonic creatures. It is also a good area for the mantas to congregate for mating. The mantas experience internal fertilization like sharks and the copulation lasts about ninety seconds. If the male is successful, in about nine-to-twelve months, a live manta will be born, being as long as four feet.

Nicky was an expert on mantas and he assured us that mantas are not aggressive unless they feel threatened. He said that they are harmless to people and indifferent to divers. He added that he had been swimming around them dozens of times, as had many of his friends and researchers, and no one ever had been attacked or hurt. He said that the mantas can have up to three hundred rows of peg-like teeth, about the size of a pin head, almost looking like scales, but the teeth are not for eating or defense, but apparently play a role in the mating process, but no one knows for sure.

We slid into the water, wearing our goggles and swim fins. We timed it perfectly and just as we reached the reef opening, about fifty mantas came silently gliding in, in varying colors of grey and black, some appearing golden, and some obvious recent new-bornes. I had learned that mantas, like sharks, have no bones, just cartilage, and this body configuration showed in their very, smooth effortless swimming. They saw us and hardly paid any attention. I dove down and looked upward, and watched their silhouettes against the sky, looking like giant bats. Every time we reached the surface for air, the sense of exhilaration was over whelming. Fortunately, being in the right place at the right time, it was viewing nature at its purest best. I enjoyed watching them swim in groups, so graceful, almost appearing like autumn leaves gently moved by the wind.

I saw several of the mantas jumping out of the water. I asked Nicky about this behavior, and he answered, "Glad you mentioned that. There have been reports of mantas attacking boats, but what happened was the boat was too close as the manta was jumping and came down on the boat, damaging the vessel and smashing the occupants."

"Why do they jump?"

Nicky answered, "For many reasons.  Sometimes they're trying to escape predators down below.  Tiger sharks are one of their main enemies.  Oftentimes they're jumping to knock the parasites off their skin.  That's very common.  Another reason that researchers have discovered and you will love this one, they might be showing off for the females in the mating period, or sometimes, it is thought, they are just being playful and doing the jumps for fun."

Jonah popped to surface real fast with his goggles missing and exclaimed, "Guys, I was swimming next to one about five feet away, when he suddenly turned towards me and bumped me big-time. That bump threw me into the path of another one, and I headed straight to the surface for escape.  I kinda felt like a ping-pong ball.  Those fish are big and strong."

Nicky laughed and said, "Oh yeah.  Good thing it wasn't tackle football!"

We all took deep breaths and dove deep again.  The mantas were in no hurry to leave, and continued to swim and feed.  As the sun set, we reluctantly made our way to the shore lights.  We hadn't planned on a night dive.  Jonah mentioned something about returning on the next night with lights and cameras and possibly doing a documentary for the Discovery Channel.  Nicky just smiled and said, "Remember your agreement and how the curse will get you if you pay too much attention to the secret spot! No publicity. You don't want to break out in massive warts, or have your pee-pee fall off , or end up as shark bait on your next dive.  These things can happen."

Jonah chuckled, "I got it, Oh Great Protector of the Mantas. You're loud and clear.  Let's go get some Mexican food to celebrate our special secret place."

I liked that choice.  Curses aren't my idea of fun but a pile of tacos and tostadas just might be...and a coupla bottles of ice-cold Coronas. It was a good day swimming with the mantas.

After the scrumptious meal and the retelling of great memories, Yancey and Sally bid us adieu and headed back to the Shark Tooth. They said they would listen for the island chatter and watch for Ignacio on their return voyages.

The local dive shops had already lined twenty new clients, mostly military guys, for diving excursions to Palau and Chuuk. With gorgeous

Sally and two new Filipina crew members aboard, the testosterone would be flying off the decks.

Yancey might have to put some clothes on his main squeeze.

# 22

---

# AT THE GUAM AIRPORT

$C$arlos and I did some last minute shopping on Guam. Saipan is beautiful and relaxing but considered ennui for dedicated shoppers like our wives. We managed to spend several hours in the main shops finding plenty of clothes and shoes. Ladies must have their many sandals and shoes for all occasions. There's no explaining it – it's just a basic principle of life, as true as the earth revolving around the sun, or water running downhill.

We arrived at the Guam airport in plenty of time for our forty-minute prop plane ride to Saipan. There had been a major reunion on Guam of former troops that had served in World War II, Korea and Vietnam. One of the local guys, Al Renaldo, knew Carlos. Al had brought his friend to the airport for his long flight back to Missouri. While on his tour of duty in Vietnam he was shot twice. He walked with a distinctive limp from being shot in the spinal area and also in his right hand. He wore his Purple Heart with pride.

Al introduced his friend, Ned, to us saying, "Ned is the last of the straight-arrows. He's one of the good guys. I'll bet that he doesn't even piss when he's in the shower." Al said that he had to get back to work to make some bucks to pay the utility bills. He had a wonderful, bizarre sense of humor, joking about being shot twice, like he didn't learn much after being shot the first time. He went back on the line and got shot again.

Al laughed and said, "My mother always told me that I was a slow learner."

We didn't want him to leave, enjoying his company, but he had several clients coming to his office.

His friend was former First Lieutenant Ned Fishman from the US Army, 52$^{nd}$ Aviation Battalion, 119$^{th}$ Aviation Company, stationed at Camp Holloway near Pleiku, Vietnam. Ned has been in the ROTC during his college years, and after graduation, had gone to flight school to fly Huey Helicopters, model UH-1B with a single turbo jet engine. Part of the training took place in Fort Sill, and as part of the informal training, meant to teach technical skills and to test one's own personal mettle. Without authorization, each pilot had to fly through a sixty-foot-wide canyon with chopper blades thirty-nine feet wide. Ned survived the training and earned his wings, and within months found himself flying an armed helicopter right smack in the war zone. There were twenty-five choppers in their unit and most of their work was within a sixty-mile radius. Every day was filled with uncertainty about what the enemy was planning.

Each helicopter carried two pilots (an extra flyboy in case one was injured), a gunner and a crew chief. The choppers were tasked to carry supplies to forward units, food, make rescues and give support to ground troops. The chopper was loaded with 2.75" rocket propelled warheads, and machine guns, Model M60 with a 7.62mm ammunition.

During a supply drop up north, a typical request came from a Green Beret Unit under attack from enemy insurgents. Ned asked for specific information and the officer answered in a clear, calm voice, "We're a little busy right now. We're under fire. Can you call me back?" Before Ned could reply, the officer added, "See that ravine over on the right – right along the tree line? See if you can light it up. We're taking lead from that area."

The machine gunners started hitting the tree line. The tracer ammunition found the mark and they headed the chopper in that direction. Ned and his fellow pilot fired off a dozen rockets, two at a time, but only one made it to the target. One rocket just stalled in the tube and immediately caught on fire. It was only five feet from Ned. He realized the thin aluminum skin of the chopper was not going to be much protection if the rocket exploded.

Training and experience paid off, and no one panicked, but they knew they couldn't land and if they headed back to base, they could blow up along the way, and if they survived, the Viet Cong didn't exactly follow the rules set up the Geneva Convention. In this terrible situation, Ned thought a hundred different solutions in a matter of seconds, but none of them seemed plausible. Finally they decided they would stay near the Green Beret camp – at least they had good medics if the rocket exploded.

Then as there was divine intervention, the rocket quit burning almost as quickly as it started. Suddenly over the radio they heard a wonderful voice from the camp, "I believe the bastards checked out. It should be safe to come in now."

Ned never saw anything specific about the effectiveness on the enemy targets, except a lot of flames and smoke. Apparently this was enough to convince the enemy to cease firing and they ran, or they were killed and injured and were carried off. On the ground, the crew tried to determine why the rocket hadn't fired like it should. They couldn't figure it but at least they were safe.

Ned and his crew were greeted with cheers in the Army camp and were able to make their supply drop with the ground troops without any further firing. Part of the delivery was mail from home, and the chopper crew members were heroes twice in one day. It was much appreciated that the ride back to the airfield was quiet and uneventful.

The hotel in their home staging area was overflowing with military and civilian guests. The Army assigned the pilots to stay at a French colonial hunting lodge near Ban Me Thuot. The rooms were laid out in some sort of complex pattern – no one knew for sure. It ws hard to navigate even when sober. On one of their liberties in town, Ned's good friend, Bobby, returned to the bar after the ten o'clock curfew and soon found himself drunk after-hours. When he stumbled home to the lodge, he went in the wrong door, and couldn't find his room on the second or third floor. On an upper floor, he walked in on a Viet Nam couple, busily engaged in finding one another's pleasure points. Embarrassed and disoriented, Bobby tried to run away through the patio and fell out onto the telephone wires. His fall was broken at the second floor, and when he crawled back in the lodge, he luckily found his room right away. Bobby was a good pilot and showed up on the flight line next day on time a wee bit haggard. The commander liked to fly with him, was sure of his competence, and made him a training instructor.

A few days later, Bobby and the commander got into an argument about base security. A small wager was made. Bobby bet that he could walk up on the Vietnamese base guards at nighttime and take away a rifle with ease. The commander disagreed, saying the guards were too sharp. Three days later, Bobby slipped off to a Vietnamese guard post in kdarkness, about seventy-five yards away, and jerked the rifle from the guard. He yelled into the camp, "I've got it!" The commander said that he couldn't see the rifle in the dark, so Bobby fired off a round into the air, bringing the entire camp to full alert. For this fiasco, the commander was relieved of his command, and returned to flying, which he preferred anyway.

When boredom and sometimes high intensity, life-threatening events took place, high jinks and goofiness were often the great stress relievers. Several weeks after the rifle incident, one of Ned's relief pilots, Orley, got his R & R at a nearby beach hamlet, a small-town saturated with GI bars and girly-girly shows. Orley voiced the goal of "searching out young maidens, breaking them in, and capturing their innocence." He hadn't quite realized that it wasn't his charm and good looks that attracted the ladies, but it was his billfold, and how many greenbacks were left after payday. The ladies were into survival and taking care of their families, or some sad cases, buying their drugs and covering their gambling losses.

When Orley didn't return to base, Ned and the MP's went looking for him. Several excited civilians said they had seen a naked American man running amok on the beach, screaming something about money and "fucking whores." He fit the description of Orley. After a lengthy search, they found him sitting on a beach rock, exhausted from running and completely naked, wearing only a condom, his little love appendage still semi-erect. They covered him with a blanket from the truck, loaded him up and headed back to base. As the story unraveled, Orley had paid a hooker for sex on the beach, and just as he got ready for the earth-shattering moment under a bright moon, the girl took off with his money and clothes, and most particularly, his honor. He was really pissed off that the little girl could outrun him. It took weeks for this story to die down back on the base. Every time it was his turn to fly, some wiseacre would yell, "Hey Lieutenant Orley. Is this flight with or without clothes?" or "Lieutenant, don't forget your raincoat protection."

At the Guam airport, our planes were an hour late, Ned's to San Francisco and our puddle-jumper to Saipan, so we had plenty of time to hear some more stories from Ned. Carlos and I shared a few "police stories" about some of our weirdest and most dangerous captures. Most didn't involve a daily death possibility from a hidden enemy.

Ned recalled a near calamity when one of the two machine guns wasn't properly pinned and locked down on a fellow pilot's chopper. The concept is that the machine guns can only swing to an angle where the projectiles won't hit the chopper walls and endanger the crew and pilots. Somehow, the pins came loose in the brackets and when the gunner started firing at the enemy, several of the bullets came back inside the chopper, and he shot himself in the buttocks and right leg. The chopper was still functional. Fortunately, no major blood vessel was hit on the gunner, and the pilot was able to maneuver out of the fire zone and get the gunner back to the hospital.

Carlos asked, "Was it ever routine. Did you ever feel safe?"

Ned said, "All it would take to bring a chopper down was a well-placed shot to the pilot's head, or a ground missile, or even a barrage of machine gun fire when we went in low to pick up the wounded and rescue the ground troops. I never felt comfortable or confident during my year's tour. In fact, I had a real fright about fifty hours before I was headed for home. We train and prepare, but it's still scary."

Ned relayed several incidents where the military guy got hit on his last week or even on the last day. Some never made it home after finishing their year of duty. In his case, he was getting packed and ready to fly to the transportation zone in Saigon. He had one more night on the lines. About midnight, the major pulled him out of his rack and said that the base was under fire, and that he needed him to get in the air and make an immediate surveillance. He and his crew cranked up, got air-borne, but didn't see any signs of enemy troops. Later investigation revealed that one of the Vietnamese soldiers had accidentally fired his rifle out near the base perimeter. There was no attack on the base but

Ned's adrenaline stayed on high alert. It was a nerve-wrenching SNAFU that stopped Ned from sleeping until he was homeward bound.

Two days later, he was on a military plane that took him to Japan and Alaska, and finally to the Travis Air Force Base in California. From there he flew to Fort Benning, Georgia where he finished out his enlistment. Shortly thereafter, he met his future bride, Camille, and the rest is a history of marital bliss, raising children, and a school teaching career.

Our planes finally arrived and it was time to wander off to our respective gates. We shook hands, said our goodbyes with promises that we would try to get to Missouri and he to Saipan. I enticed him with a few more fishing stories about the Northern Marianas Islands. I told him about the Marianas Trench Marine National Monument that would protect the waters and islands of Asuncion, Maug and Uracas, encompassing about 115,000 square miles of ocean.

Vietnam vets are mostly in their twilight years but Ned still walked strong and tall and looked every bit a military officer.

Carlos said, "Looking strack for an old-timer. The man did his duty and makes us proud."

"So true. That's why we call them warriors!"

# 23

## TIME FOR FISHING

For the next two weeks, Carlos and I continued to track the funds in Ignacio's personal account with the Bank of Guam. There had been no activity, not even a tiny withdrawal.

The designated funds had been received by Ignacio's family in California, and Saipan had been enriched by over three million dollars. The Legislative had a little difficulty in deciding how much money should go Rota, Tinian and Saipan, but finally managed to divvy up the money sensibly as needed, based on population, with equal shares to education, health and medical, and the senior citizens. Two of the more belligerent senators resorted to fisticuffs, but the fight soon ended when both of the out-of-shape, obese men decided to call it a draw; and they withdrew to the beach with a case of ice-cold cerveza and canned meat sandwiches on white bread. Of course, afterwards they broke out the betel nut and spit red saliva on the white, sandy beach. Diabetes candidates waiting to happen.

Our fee had been successfully transferred to the Investigations Agency account, and the hotel accountant, Mario II, was researching the best way to invest the money. Stocks didn't seem to be a good idea at this stage.

On the third week, I heard Carlos yell from his office, "He's alive. He made it. He began making withdrawals on Pohnpei this week, just small amounts, enough to buy some rice and chicken. The bank verified it's him on the ATM camera."

"The old bastard made it to his island hideaway.  Good for him. Now he can live happily ever after."

"The easy-going life will probably add another ten years to his longevity if he remembers to exercise and give up the smokes."

The phone rang. Carlos picked it up, and started smiling. He said, "Yeah, yeah," several times, and closed by saying, "That's great! We'll pick you up.  Tom and Cocina will have a room for you folks."

I asked, "Who was that?"

"You won't believe it. Big surprise.  Ned got home, told his wife about the islands, and the good life, and the fishing. He told her about the warm climate and how orchids can't stop growing out here."

"And…" Cocina walked into the office.

"They're coming out for a month.  They're already in Guam and will be here in about two hours."

She asked, "Is that the flyboy you told me about?"

"Yep, that's him.  He brought his wife with him.  They've been married for over forty years."

Cocina called Myla at the desk, and had a room prepared on the top floor with an astounding view of the Philippines Sea.

I called my brother, Zeke Parker, up on the north end of the island and asked him to find his partner Arnie Arizapa, and get the fishing boat ready.  The "big ones" were about to do battle with a determined angler from the Midwest.

We found Ned, and his wife Camille, at the Saipan Airport, and brought them back to the hotel.  She was a beautiful woman who obviously took good care of herself and faithfully did her exercises.  She and Cocina hit it off right away, and they were soon walking through the hotel orchid garden and talking about shopping and recipes. They walked through Kaylene Mendoza's small clothing factory at the hotel where she made her cowboy and aloha shirts.  Camille bought two shirts for Ned, and two blouses for herself.  The patterns were bright and colorful, with flowers, canoes, guitars, palm trees, hula girls and island warriors.  Carlos often said that he came from good DNA and the ferocious looking guapo warrior in the pattern was copied from his father.

Ned and Camille were overwhelmed by the location of their room, high enough to catch a late afternoon breeze from Mount Topochau and to watch the boats and jet skis out in the lagoon. They showered up and threw on some aloha clothes to be comfortable. For sunset dinner, Guangman had prepared a typical feast of local delicacies, including pork adobo, red rice and plenty of fresh veggies and fruits. He prepared a special cassava pudding for dessert and a plate of tasty purplish taro.

Zeke and Arnie arrived for an after-dinner cognac and to do some planning for the fishing expedition. Ned told them he didn't want them to go any special trouble, but they soon assured him that it was time to go fishing, not only for him but the hotels were getting short of the open ocean deep-water fish like mahi-mahi, yellow fin tuna and barracuda. One of the hotels asked them to catch some more shark for their specialty menu. The front of the hotel's menu read "Out in the ocean, the shark eats you...but here in our restaurant, you eat the shark." On the front of the menu there was a cartoon showing the customer munching on a shark with a bubble caption from the shark, "Yikes!"

Next morning the boat and crew were ready, and so was Marcella, still attired in her fancy fishing duds with about twenty pockets on her pants and khaki vest, and they all seemed to be bulging with necessities. She was feeling mighty chipper –Zeke had just named the fishing boat after her *The Pretty Lady*. The red paint ws barely dry on the white hull. The fishing crew was taking Ned and Camille up north to Maug and Uracus and would be gone for almost ten days. They expected fair sailing but were close enough to several of the islands that if bad weather hit, they could find safety in a protected lagoon. Arnie was a conservative sailor and wouldn't hesitate to take shelter and wait out a storm.

Ned had noticed the "13 Fishermen Monument" on Beach Road and asked what had happened and who were the fishermen.

Arnie winced and said, "It was a very sad event and didn't have to happen, and thirteen lives were lost at sea. This incident involved the single greatest loss of life in the Commonwealth of the Northern Marianas Island since World War II. This was one case where they should have listened to the weatherman.

"On September 19, 1986, the fishing vessel *M/V Olwol* left Saipan to go commercial fishing in the Northern Islands with a total of thirteen men aboard. There were storm warnings, the approach of a possible typhoon, but the captain decided he could outrun the storm. However, Typhoon Ben, Condition 1, followed their course, and circled around the fishing boat as it neared Agrihan Island, and struck with a vengeance with 100 MPH winds. The captain radioed both Agrihan and Pagan Island, and said that he was in trouble with high waves and that he was headed for a safe harbor on Pagan Island. However, the ship and crew never made it. A massive search was undertaken when the winds calmed.

"It was not until September 26, seven days later, that a Coast Guard plane spotted the *Olwol* upside down, bouncing in the waves off of Maug Island. Divers were dispatched but found no survivors or bodies but did recover personal items such as suitcases, back packs and a wallet belonging to one of the crew members."

Camille commented, "A real tragedy. It must have affected many families."

Arnie continued, "It was terrible times for the island families, especially for the Carolinian parents. Except for the captain and a Filipino mechanic, most of the men were teenagers or in their early twenties. They went along for the adventure and a share of the catch. About half of the crew had been fishing up north three-to-four times, so they weren't exactly novices on the sea."

Ned inquired, "Did the search continue, like maybe on the mountainous interior of the islands?"

"Sure, for about six months. Volunteers kept combing the islands looking for any signs of habitation and life. The military and Coast Guard continued to do periodic flights." He quietly added, " A very sad story."

Before *The Pretty Lady* hoisted anchor for the fishing expedition, Guangman and his family appeared with a gigantic healthy lunch, plus refrigerated containers filled with loads of food prepared for the next few days. After that they would have to depend on each other for cooking and the boat's stores, and all the fresh fish they could catch and eat.

Zeke said, "We might have to punish you once in a while, and serve giant crabs and lobsters."

Ned answered good-naturedly, "Hurt us if you must." He paused and asked, "Hey, do we get a cut of the profits if we get a good catch?"

Zeke answered, "Sounds okay to me but first we deduct the fuel costs, wear-and-tear on the boat and motor, and big bucks for Marcella's good meals. Come to think of it, you might be owing us a lot of money!"

Ned smiled and declared, "Forget I ever asked. Let's go fishing!"

Zeke unhooked the lines and off they went northbound with Arnie at the controls. I said to Cocina, "There goes a happy bunch. Let's hope those landlubbers don't get seasick."

"I gave Camille two packets of motion sickness pills. She said they usually didn't get seasick but when I told her about the eight-foot rolling swells, she stashed the pills quickly in her purse and said, "Just in case. It doesn't look ladylike to be barfing over the side hour after hour."

I laughed and said, "Cocina, you remember your first long trip?"

"Hey, that was just once, and only because you put too many jalapeno peppers in the breakfast eggs."

"Yeah, and you rid of the toxins in your body on that trip. You tossed out a unique rainbow of colors from your guts. I had never seen those colors before."

"Both ends, too. Damn, I was sick but only on that one day, drank some water and got fresh air, and I adjusted to the motion. The next three days were smooth-sailing."

"Oh, I remember that. You kept pulling me down below for an afternoon delight, and all I wanted to do was troll for marlin."

"Then your body was lying, Big Boy. I remember the little soldier didn't give a hoot about fishing anymore."

"He was fishing in his own sneaky, evil way."

"And what a catch! That was a good day."

By radio we heard the weather for the north fishing expedition had been mild, but the boat was about three hours late getting back to the hotel. Cocina hadn't started to worry yet. When we finally spotted it on the horizon, the boat was flying a "marlin flag" from the mast. Ned had the big catch of the day – a 425 pound marlin he had snagged about ten miles off the Saipan coast and it took almost four hours to bring it aboard. The boat was loaded down with a vast assortment of fish for the hotels and for Guangman's menus, and Ned had plenty enough for the smoker oven and to take home in his luggage.

Zeke and Arnie had shown the crew where the *Olwol* had disappeared. Camille said, "It seemed so lonely and desolate up there, and so far from their loved ones."

I commented, "A sad account for sure. Most of the young boys would be their forties by now, probably with their own families and ready to be grandpas."

The month's visit flew by and Ned and Camille reluctantly packed up and got ready for the airport. We had shown them the permanent apartments at the hotels, and as we watched them hunker down on the decks in the big comfy chairs, Cocina said, "They'll be back, at least for another visit. Camille loved the ocean. She talked about bringing out their grandbabies."

I smiled and said, "You know what? I love the ocean too, but I think I love you more." He nudged against her and brushed his lips against her ear.

"Easy, Big Fella. You are a sweetie but remember, we're having dinner with Ned and Camille in thirty minutes."

"Plenty enough time, and you look so exquisite in the sunset with embarrassed, flushed cheeks."

"Newly weds forever."

# 24

---

# THE POWER OF SUGGESTION

We're all susceptible to suggestion and possibility. All an observer has to do is check out the ads on television or in the magazines. We're immediately attracted by a sexy feline, or in the lady's case by the young lad with well-defined abs, and if the sexy person is selling a car or a special cologne, we can almost put yourself in the photo, especially behind the wheel of that car with that new-car smell. If nothing else, we are attracted to the product or the situation or a special place to travel like Asia or particularly Saipan. We pay attention. Why do you suppose they usually have beautiful, swaying hula girls on the travel posters and in the travel magazines?

Along with the power of suggestion is the confusion or recklessness of human communication, sometimes called gossip or "one-upmanship," when telling a story. Remember that fun game in Psyche 101 class, where the class members would sit in a circle of chairs, and Student A would whisper to Student B, and so on, until the story or message made the circular journey and got back to the originator? Then the written original message would be compared to the final version of the message. Oftentimes the ending message was off in leftfield, or non- discernible, or unrelated to the written message.

The islands are beautiful and quiet, but often boring for some of my friends. Sometimes we have to make our own fun and excitement. Conservative Accountant Brent decided to have some fun with the little fairy creatures (called menehunes in Hawaii) that supposedly live in the jungle. Most all local island people, and the Filipinos, believe in these magical entities that allegedly reside in deep forests and hidden valleys. These little characters are a cross between a witch (*bruja* in the Philippines) and a leprechaun, or possibly a ghost, but most, if not all, are friendly but they often scare the dickens out of you when they appear out of nowhere. Plus they are unpredictable like an A.D.D. patient (Attention Deficit Disorder), sometimes attentive and other times totally hyperactive, impulsive and doing mischievous things. They have no regular home and like to reside on creeper vines and sometimes in limestone caves. Like UFO's, they're often spotted during full moon phases, or by some drunkard who just left the corner pub, or an escapee from the looney bin.

Over a period of several months, Brent started stacking rocks on one another like a cairn, some small, some large, and in some areas, the limestone rocks always numbered six and other places, just three or four. He did the little piles all along the favorite walking trails of Saipan, and soon, some people were explaining to tourists that cairns are old legend markers, that some were part of an old Chamorro worship tradition, and that forest creatures like to do the markers as an artistic endeavor. The dozens of the little rock piles finally made the newspapers and television with great photos by enthusiastic photographers, some with the sun setting through the cairns like some ancient version of Stonehenge.

Brent usually did his mischief right at daybreak so very few people were out and about during his rock stacking. It was reported that some American man (fitting Brent's description) was seen piling up rocks at sunrise, but the partner of this observer simply said, "I saw him too, but I think he was just straightening out the pile. Maybe the last storm knocked them down. Those markers have been there for centuries." Of course, the cairns had only been there for several weeks or months.

Suffice to say, the markers are still in place and gradually expanding in numbers and height. The local people believe the little jungle creatures are multiplying into family groups and getting more creative with their artwork. The Asian tourists love the stories.

About a week later after seeing the commotion caused by the cairns, another friend ex-state trooper Wayne, started placing six-inch red stars on telephone poles and on bulletin boards at department stores.

The following week, making sure that the person had departed for the mainland and wasn't on island, he would place a first name only under the star in bold print. To most people without checking, it was assumed that the named person had just disappeared. Ten days later, he drove a rusty knife into a telephone pole on a busy intersection. The police were actually called when a citizen spotted the knife. The island chatter started right away, when "Henry" or "Freddie" or "Chico" couldn't be found anywhere, and similar names were on the poles. Suspicion of foul play began to circulate. The CIA was mentioned, that maybe the missing people had actually been in a witness protection program, or maybe, just maybe, they had crossed someone in the organization and been dumped on the other side of the reef.

The next week, Wayne added several more stars and more names, but this time he left on two different poles some old black pants that SWAT members wear and some water-faded and ripped official ID's. The following week, he added large pink stars and listed ladies' names. Now when "Kathy" or "Lucia" or "Jessie" couldn't be found, foul play was not only suspected, but it was argued that maybe one of the gals ran off with one of the missing men in some sort of romantic entanglement These suspicious circumstances also made the newspaper and television. Some of it was cleared up when relatives realized that if "The Phantom" (he earned a media name) was nailing up stars with the names of their son or daughter and they knew their offspring had gone off to college or started a new job, and they were safe and accounted for.

But because of the excitement and the power of suggestion, the gossip continued for several months and the stars kept appearing. On one pole, the police found a hatchet and on another, two large fishing hooks with heavy sinkers. About this same time, a missing fisherman, who had been swept off the rocks by a freak wave, was found and his fishing line was wound around his neck and he had a fishing hook lodged in his eye cavity. He had been fishing in an area forbidden to visit according to ancient tradition. It was even more confusing because his name of Dante had not been listed on a star on a telephone pole. Brent couldn't pass this one up with the consternation and confusion; and he managed in darkness to build a cairn where the man was swept into the ocean, and then another cairn where his body was discovered.

After several months, the stars stopped appearing on the poles. No one ever realized that Wayne had taken a job in Texas and had moved. Through a sense of justice and frivolity, Brent had managed to place Wayne's star and name on the telephone pole in front of the main police and fire buildings. Wayne was never identified as "The Phantom," and of course, even though there were no more stars, the star stories have continued to unfold. No copy-cat star makers have appeared yet.

It is rumored that the police intend to stake out the trails for the cairn-builder, but that will never happen. The cops would have to get up too early in the morning and besides if they anger the little jungle people, who knows what might happen!

Better to be safe… and let Brent do his work. He came to realize that the spin-off to this farce was a lot of walking and bending over and carrying rocks, resulting in a flatter abdomen and the loss of ten pounds. He's got most of the trails finished, but if he worked on the beaches, he could well lose another ten pounds.

# 25

## A DAY AT "UGLY ELMER'S" RESTAURANT

Occasionally I like to mosey into other restaurants and try out the menus, and Ugly Elmer's is one of my favorite spots. They still serve food the old-fashioned way with lots of grillwork and grease. Owner Elmer Jones wouldn't know the difference between diesel fuel or peanut butter oil, as long as it tasted good on burgers, bacon and sausage, and fried eggs. The grits are all tasty smothered in catsup, local boonie peppers and Tabasco. He's a lovable old codger, retired navy and the tattoos to prove it, and is one ugly son-of-bitch with three front teeth missing and the ones remaining stained with nicotine. He generally sports a week's growth of beard, and a dirty "kiss the cook" apron. If you wanted to describe a person that had left his own people and stayed too long on a remote island, that's Elmer's listing in the encyclopedia.

Smoking isn't allowed in Saipan restaurants, only on the outside, like a garden area with picnic tables. Elmer got around that requirement by cutting a large hole in one of the walls, put in large yucca plant next to the window, and declared it outside. If it rains and blows hard, he just lowers a large shutter.

I like his place because of him and his sense of humor, and also the colorful island characters that bounce in and out. He gets a lot of

transients that travel from island to island, wearing out their welcome
on one isle, and then moving on to the next. As long as they have money
to pay their bills, and he's careful not ask the origin of the moolah,
everyone is welcome, unless you're really scroungy and annoying the
other customers with your hideous body odors. He keeps an outside
bath tub just for that reason that gets its water from a rain catchment. If
you don't pass the "smell test," out you go to get sanitized in rainwater.
Some of the waitresses do double duty for extra cash and will take time
out to wash clothes, give hair cuts and shaves, and it has been rumored
that they give special "happy ending" massages.

One of the regular customers is a middle-aged Filipino amigo named
Pepito De Oro. Everyone kids him about his name, "Oro" meaning
gold in Espanol, and sometimes he has money to throw around and
buys lunch for everyone. He's a chronic gambler. Mostly he's broke
and for several years, he seemed to be losing much of his anatomy. On
one month's absence, he came back after visiting with his family in the
Philippines, and was missing three fingers on his left hand. He said he
had a boating accident. Another time, he came back with a large scar
on his side, and said that he had to have a kidney removed because of
an infection. On his last visit, he walked into the restaurant, wearing
new clothes and wearing an eye patch. He bought everyone a meal and
I noticed he had a thick roll of cash. I figured eye transplants in the
Manila hospital paid mucho pesos.

My curiosity "need to know" took over. During a lull in storytelling
and general braggadocio, I pulled Pepito over to a private corner. I said,
"Amigo, what the hell are you doing in the PI? Are you really selling
your body parts?"

"Yeah, some parts; but how did you know? There's a big demand
in the Makati medical centers, no questions asked."

"Hell, that's easy to figure out. You go to Manila broke, and you
come back flush with money, but missing a part of your body."

"I'm thinking about selling a lung and maybe some more fingers."

"Pepito, you've got to beat the gambling habit – too much poker and
jueding. Get your life together. You're a house painter by trade – damn
it, start painting again. If you sell a lung, you won't be able to stand the
fumes and the hard work of climbing ladders and walking on roofs."

"You're probably right. My sister thinks I've gone loco. She's taking me to a counselor tomorrow."

"Bueno, now go home and save the money you have left." I watched him leave, hoping that he would make it to the counselor and bypass all the poker arcades.

Another regular came strolling in, shoulders slumped and head down. His name is Stu Arconit, a likeable fellow, but can have you depressed in less than ten minutes if you listened to all his woes of his world – a real ditherer and sometimes, a pain in the ass. He's a retired school teacher and was planning on moving to Missouri to do a little farming. His wife of twenty-six years wasn't enthused about living on a farm, or being old, and after cleaning out their bank accounts, took off with a young surfer, and her last post card was from Adelaide, Australia. The card simply said, "Don't worry. I'm enjoying all the good wines, and Chino (my surfer boy) has me riding the waves. Love from your good friend, Joyce. (well, not always good, sometimes very BAD!)."

He showed me the post card. The front had a glorious photo of a buffed surfer dude, with bleached blonde hair, wearing a skimpy bikini bottom with an enviable bulging package, and a puka shell necklace. I read the message. She was definitely "kicking sand in his face."

Stu said, "These little notes drive me crazy, makes me depressed. I can picture her riding more than waves. I keep seeing her on top of him."

I asserted, "Young Foolish Man, women make changes, and maybe she's chasing rainbows, maybe missing her courting days and wants to be laid by a different guy. Who knows? She might not even know herself; but now you have to make some big changes in your life. You're already told me that you don't want another wife, which by the way, I've heard that from plenty of guys who get married again, so you need to find some techniques to get her out of your worry zone. Maybe you need to create some new dynamite memories, and maybe you need someone to be riding you. You have to make life happen. Just don't take what falls your way. How about climbing the Himalayas, or floating down the Amazon River? Palawan in the Philippines is close and you could explore the hidden caverns."

"I think you're right, but I don't want anything too dangerous and ending up in a wheelchair. I know I don't want something in the romance department on a permanent basis."

"I know what you need – a trip to Bangkok and meet some ladies. A trip downtown can make a hard man humble in just one night. Go to the Nana Plaza."

He smiled and said, "I've heard about the beautiful women there. A guy in the bar last week told me that if I could find an ugly-looking woman in Thailand, he'd give a hundred bucks."

"Stu, my Boy. There's your challenge. You've got the time and money. The plane leaves every day."

"You know any bars there?"

"I was there several years back and remember three fun bars, Stud Farm, Infinity, and Illicit Memories; but the bars come and go, just like the ladies. Ask some of the young lads here today. They'll know the latest joints."

While I was talking again to Elmer, Stu was going from table to table, writing little notes on a pad. He was animated and walking straighter. He had a mission.

Elmer said, "I wonder if the therapists ever use your methods to treat their patients. A slight mention of a Thai woman seemed to perk him right up."

I looked out the front window and saw another island character, Mickey Carter, walking from a hotel, waving back at an older Japanese lady. She looked like she was still in her kimono. He had two boonie dogs on leashes and was coming to the restaurant. Mickey was a professional beach boy, handsome, had little education and never even considered getting a job. He tied his dogs next to the large window that represented the outside smoking area.

Mickey said to the waitress, "Emily, please get me the largest, hotter cheeseburger you have, and a humongous plate of fries and some red onions. I am one hungry hombre."

Elmer said, "You got money? You can't be freeloading around here. I gotta pay my staff and pay the fucking power bill."

"You take Japanese yen?" He pulled out a crisp ten thousand yen note.

"If the money is real, I'll take Egyptian pounds or Nepalese rupees… and of course, Japanese yen."

"Then in that case Emily, make it a winning trifecta of cuisine. You better add a salad to my burger and fries, just to make sure I get my nourishment and fiber."

I asked, "Where you get that kind of money?" After the words flew out of my mouth, I realized how naïve I was and how silly the question was.

He smiled and nodded his head back towards the Japanese lady's hotel. "She was on the beach and I just walked my dogs past her. You know my shtick. The one boonie dog, Sweetheart, ran over to her and started rubbing against her leg. She had never touched a dog before and when the petting started, the other mutt joined in. She gave them some snacks. She gave me a cold beer out of her little icebox. I showed her how the mutts chased sticks in the ocean and she threw the stick a coupla times."

Elmer said, "That easy, eh?"

"This one was particularly easy. She was alone and speaks a bit of English but if there's another woman, they can't make up their minds who might want go with me. If one goes with me, the other one will hold a big secret for back home. Also this one is older and hot to go while she's on vacation. Back in California, we'd call her a "cougar," looking for a younger man, even a guy in his late teens. By occupation, she's a bank manager and there's lots of yen in her purse."

"How do you get some of that yen in your pocket? She obviously savvy and not a dummy."

"That's also easy. I know that she doesn't want to pay for sex and I know she's horny; and most vacationing ladies want an adventure to remember, even if it's kinda wrong or over the limit. So I come up with a story that I needed rent money because I lost my job with the downturn of the economy. She gave me the ten thousand yen to help out. Then, if she invites me back, I know that everything will be good for the whole week while she's here."

Elmer asked, "Did you get your invite?"

"Yep, tomorrow night at nine o'clock. She has an official dinner meeting with some other bankers but said she would be home by that time. She asked me to wait in the lobby until she got back."

Elmer inquired, "And how was the sex?   She's an old dame, right?"

"Yeah, she's old for me, about forty I would say; but not for you guys.  She takes good care of herself, goes to the gym regular."

I had to ask, "You didn't say anything about the sex?"

He grinned, sitting back like an old sage on the mountain, "You old men know.  The secret of life is pussy.  Before being born, we struggle to get out, and then the rest of our lives, we're trying to get back in. All sex is good. She's satisfied and I'm very happy."

There was a lot of truth in that statement, and Mickey had learned it early on. Add tons of love, a nice home, a tasty meal and good health. What else is there?

His words even held more truth when Stu got back from Thailand. Two weeks later, he walked into the restaurant standing tall, belly pulled in, with a glint in his eyes. His self-confidence and charisma were overwhelming, lighting up the room

I said, "Looks like it went okay?"

"Oh yeah!  I've discovered life again!"

"Is the ex-wife Joyce out of your brain now?"

"Joyce?  Who the fuck is Joyce?"

# EPILOGUE

$A$nd there you have it. You met more island interesting characters and enjoyed their stories vicariously, plus another major case solved. Most of the government money had been returned and the former governor was out of office, probably lounging and fishing on some remote tropical island. He's better off living on an anodyne beach in open spaces, doing what he always wanted to do, and not living in some grey concrete jail at the taxpayer's expense, and complaining about the same dinner menu every week.

Island life is full of memories of good times, with the bad and unpleasant just fading away into the past. Today eclipses yesterday, and moves us forward to the morrow with splendid opportunities. One day blends into the next, an idyllic existence, and I suppose it has been that way for centuries on our little rock.

The island experience can be easy-living at its best, or can be very dangerous. In one direction you can see a postcard perfect vista and to describe it as "awesome" is an understatement. Go to the other side of the island, you can see huge waves slapping on flat table stones and in a second, a renegade wave could sweep the unaware fisherman off into the deep Pacific Marianas Trench. We live...then we die. What we do in between is important. The whole concept of life is puzzling, and there are a million questions about the inevitable and the aftermath. Religion and spiritual beliefs help us through the day and keeps us breathing and working, and preparing for the next dimension. It's good to spend the middle part, between birth and death, living where and how we want to live. That middle part for me is beautiful Saipan, with warm balmy breezes and swaying palm trees, fishing and hiking, and being where I want to be. I've forgotten the meanings of *could have, would have and should have.*

Besides improving our hotel accommodations for the seniors, we have created a special (*salus per aqua*) spa area which tourists now expect when they travel. The spa has become the cornerstone of global travel, which emphasizes personal beauty and health; and the original and soothing design at the Beach Hotel has become a regular story in travel magazines and web sites.

Cocina is still a champion at *philematology* and continues to be romantic and fun. She knows the full value of a lingering smooch and the endless summers of interlabial osculation spit-swapping lip-locks. She's a great kisser and a wonderful friend and lover.

We're enjoying the management of our hotel, and working with the motivated staff; and experiencing every day miracles. Nothing compares to watching the little, happy face of child who just learned to swim, or watching a transplanted West Indian soursop seed grow into a fruit-bearing tree in just a few years, or evaluating our profit margin and knowing that we can pass along some of the earnings to the staff. We also have to boast about Yoshi, with his nurturing touch, winning a recent orchid showing with the hotel orchids; and Kaylene selling her creative "cowboy shirts" all over Texas and New Mexico. Guangman is still creating magnificent, lo-calorie memorable meals, and the Beachologist can be heard strumming his uke at the high water mark, surrounded by several children, three or four jungle mutts of questionable lineage, and his attractive Chinese wife and their babies.

Carlos and I are still solving perplexing crimes and snaring the bad guys - definitely "chicken soup" for the policeman's soul. There's little in the universe that compares to the satisfying sound of the clinking metal door when the asshole gets locked up and some victim can breathe easier.

This evening I'm at beachside sitting in the warm sand at surf line. Unlike the sun that rises and sets dramatically, the moon appears silently and disappears quietly. On this peaceful twilight, I can hear the sea whispering, "Watch out, the tide is rising…better move back." And the beauty of island life is that you can come and hear your own song and write your unique poetry.

How long can paradise and the good life last? *Bahala na ang Diyos!*

# GLOSSARY

**Aso kalye** – street dog, wild, stray (Filipino)
**Chili** – penis (Chamorro)
**Credo quia absurdum** – "I believe it because it is absurd"
**Bahala na ang Diyos** – up to God (Filipino)
**Basura** – garbage, trash (Filipino – Chamorro)
**Bula-bula** – untruthful, boastful (Filipino)
**Cassava** - tapioca
**Billabong** – stagnant backwater, swamp (Australian)
**Empanada** – deep fried pastry with meat or veggies inside
**Guapo** – macho, strong and masculine, handsome (Filipino)
**Gutvik** – German slang, meaning a good fuck
**Guten morgen** – good morning (German)
**Jueding** – lotto (Filipino)
**Kamote** – sweet potatoes, eat potato and tops
**Kancun** – leafy vegetable like spinach
**Kaselehlia** – hello, aloha (Ponapeian)
**Kava** – narcotic pepper root, sakau on Pohnpei
**Maganda** – beautiful, pretty (Filipino)
**Maitresse-en-titre** – official royal mistress (French)
**Maganda** – pretty, beautiful (Filipino)
**Mondo bizarro** – very weird, strange (slang)
**Mundungus** - - smelly, bad odor, unclean guts (Spanish)
**Mwoakilloa** – Mokil, a Ponapeian island
**Nahnmwarki** – high chief, royalty, king (Ponapeian)
**Nahs** – outside hut, usually with palm fronds for a roof

(Ponapeian)

**Palayaw** –nickname (Filipino)

**Papalatong** – bullshit, phoniness, embellishment (Filipino slang)

**Philematology** – the science of kissing

**Puputa** – drunk, high, intoxicated (Ponapeian)

**Que sera sera** – whatever, that's the way it is (French)

**RIF**- reduction in force, laying off personnel

**Salus per aqua** – acronym for spa - health through water (Latin)

**Sapwuahfik** – Ngatik, a Ponapeian island

**Sashimi** – fresh fish, usually eaten with soy sauce, onions, chili, wasabi

**Schutzenfest** – military picnic, piece of cake, no problem (German)

**Sogu** – Korean liquor

**Sushi** – rice wrapped in seaweed with meats and sauces, served in small rolls

**Teufel hunden** – devil dogs, tough fighters (German)

**Trifecta** – triple, bettor picks first three finishers in exact order, hat-trick

**Yokoso** – traditional Japanese welcome